Reunion at Fortuny Bay

BOOK ONE OF FORTUNY BAY SERIES

ARA GRIGORIAN

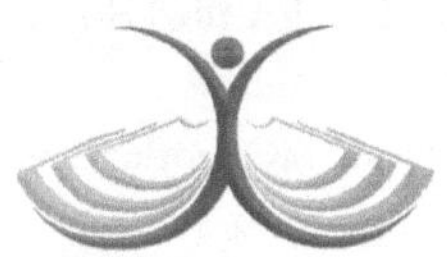

Printed in the United States of America

First Edition, 2022 - Love Laugh Learn Media

Paperback ISBN-13: 978-1-7324621-4-4
Hardcover ISBN-13: 978-1-7324621-5-1

Covert Art by Virtually Possible Designs

www.AraGrigorian.com

The team that transforms our house into a home:
Delia, Anthony, Michael

Thank you, Jesus ~ for all You've done, all You're doing, and for all that's to come. All for Your glory.

Reunion
at
FORTUNY BAY

Chapter One

Leo

Leo Moncrieff maneuvered his new convertible through the winding coastal roads that he could never forget, despite years spent erasing this town from his memories. The high beams lit up the picturesque path, and the sound of crashing waves completed the sensory overload. He was definitely back home.

'Welcome to Fortuny Bay,' the overhead sign claimed.

Was he welcome? He had not been to this town for a good... what? Seven, maybe eight years? Not much had changed. The place was still dead.

"What is this place?"

He turned to the source of the slurring voice. He'd almost forgotten about her. His new friend, Amber, had just awakened from a nap. She scanned the area like she'd just tasted something vile.

He handed her the half-finished *Dom Pérignon Rosé*. "Drink," he said.

She smiled and slurped down a few hundred dollars worth of champagne.

Leo was not about to explain to her why they'd come here. Instead, he punched the pedal, shooting the Ferrari Spider past a few flashing red lights that hung from span wires. The lights swayed gently from the strong coastal winds. He took a deep breath, inhaling the humid, salty air.

Place even smells the same.

Another left turn, and he reached the real reason he'd come here in the first place. His father.

As he slowed the car to a crawl, the engine grumbled like a wild tigress ready to pounce. He came to a complete stop in front of his father's home—*Casa Moncrieff*. The place he'd called home for the first eighteen years of his life.

Crickets and waves provided the background music to this stand-off. He stared at the old house. The place was falling apart. Surprisingly, a dim light flickered from inside the house. *Is the old man watching T.V.?* At this hour? Didn't seem possible. The man was military through and through. Slept by 10 p.m. and was up before the first rays of the sun cracked the California coastal horizon.

He put the car in park and placed his hand on the door handle. He breathed in and out, hoping to harness the same courage and killer instinct he used when making multi-million dollar decisions. Just as he was about to pop the door open, a silhouette appeared behind the drapes.

"Someone you know?" Amber asked.

Whoever was on the other side of the window was not his father. His dad was a stocky Frenchmen. That silhouette was not stocky at all. The drape separated slightly.

Had the old man sold the house? This house that had been in the family for over one-hundred years. Would his father sell Leo's genera-tional right without telling Leo? Sure, he would. He didn't owe Leo anything.

Instantly, all the courage he'd built up drained right out. He dropped the car into first and slammed the pedal, riding the clutch momentarily, peeling out and spitting out some gravel.

"Yeah!" Amber yelled. "Let's go!"

He released the clutch and they roared away. The force of the beast slapped a smile on his face. And the adrenalin rush helped him forget what he'd almost done.

That was stupid.

And childish.

To what end?

It didn't matter anymore. The game was over. Leo had won.

"Are we gonna party now?" Amber asked and placed her hand high on his thigh.

He glanced at her and grinned. "Be careful what you ask for."

She smiled that seductive smile that had gotten his attention the night before at the benefit. "I have no fear," she said.

He believed her.

Chapter Two

Leo
Two Years Later

The video feed from the conference call faded to black.

In a matter of minutes, the acquisition of one of Leo Moncrieff's technologies would be official. Gaming Kings, one of the the world's largest brick and mortar and online gambling companies would own Vitruvian's ground-breaking adaptive A.I. technology along with all its patents.

In near perfect unison, Leo, Chris Webb, and Anna Woods leaned back into their chairs and breathed out. The fishbowl conference room's glass walls had been switched to opaque to keep details of the call from all others at the Vitruvian offices.

The 85-inch video conferencing screen refreshed and a question from service the provider popped up on the screen.

Chris chuckled as he read the question. "How would you rate the quality of the call?"

Leo grinned. A very appropriate question.

"Well," Chris said. "Let me give you four-point-three-billon reasons why the quality of the call was epic."

A notepad flew from Anna, hitting Chris. "You are such a geek," she said.

"Yes, and you're the one who told me, and the geeks shall inherit the world."

"That's not how it goes," Anna said. "The meek, not geek."

"Same difference," Chris said.

"Why do I even bother?" she said, exasperated.

"Are you guys done?" Leo asked. "Can we for just a minute behave like serious—"

"Seriously rich," Chris injected.

Leo took his notepad and tossed it at Chris too.

"Enough with the abuse," Chris said.

Leo loved his friends. Yes, Leo was the ideas guy. Big, crazy, unrealistic ideas that no sane person would even consider. But every ideas guy needed the tech wizard. That was where his friend and Chief Technology Officer, Chris, came in. Chris, with his All-American longish blond hair and blue eyes would never be mistaken for a gamer or a math nerd. But he was that and much more. They had met on a gaming server when they were both still in high school. Later, they became college dorm roommates. Microsoft had offered him a job straight out of high school. But his parents convinced him to focus on his education instead. One year in and he agreed to drop out of college with Leo to be a part of Leo's vision.

"Did that really just happen?" Anna asked, as she tucked a long strand of her auburn hair behind her ear.

He turned to Anna, Leo's Chief of Staff. That was her official title, but her actual role was his lifesaver, organizational goddess, sounding board, and personal therapist. Yes, she was also the one who got things done, led the teams, used her law degree to go to war when needed, but what really mattered to him was that she was the closest thing to family.

Their story become part of Silicon Valley folklore. She had been his favorite barista at the Java and Juice coffee house in the early days. Leo had offered her the third job at his first startup. She explained that she was in her final year of law school on scholarship. He told her the world needed fewer lawyers and more leaders.

She said yes five years ago, and as soon as the sale cleared escrow, she and Chris would become very wealthy twenty-something-year-olds.

Leo ran his hands through his longish black hair, then took a deep breath and smiled. "Yeah, Anna. That really just happened."

"Un-freaking-real," Chris whispered, then turned to Leo. "You did it. Everything you promised, and everything you said we'd do, we did."

Anna bumped his shoulder with hers. "Don't let it get to your head."

Leo studied her. "Thanks, Mom. I'll have you know I'm a very humble guy. I am probably the most humble person I know. I've asked everyone who works for me and they agree."

They all chuckled, but something about her comment landed and bore into his chest. His mom had always told him the same. 'You have a gift. Stay humble, Leo. Don't get ahead of yourself.' He was grateful for the reminder. How he wished his mom had been alive to witness this day.

Anna grinned. "Let's be honest—you really can't take credit for any of this. I mean, you'd be lost without me."

"She's sort of right," Chris said. "She is the Pepper Potts to your Tony Stark."

"Not," she said. "I mean... no offense. I love you and all, but only in a pain-in-the-butt-brother type of way."

"No offense taken," Leo said. He turned to Chris. "So in this scenario, are you Tony Stark's chauffeur?"

"No, Sir. I am JARVIS," he declared with pride.

"Enough," Anna said. "This conversation very quickly entered deep into geek territory. I can't be party to that."

"Back to being cool. We need to celebrate," Leo said. "Anna, call an all-hands, say, an hour. First, we announce this deal to the rest of the team. I want them to know we're selling the tech, not the company. Also, call in the jet to Vegas for the three of us. Tonight we celebrate."

She hesitated. Her mouth parted as if to say something but stopped herself.

"What is it?" Leo asked.

She shook her head. "It's nothing. I'll take care of it."

Leo studied her but couldn't read her face. Was she worried that he'd make another poor choice? He was not about to get himself drunk like *that* again. He had no interest in spending another night at the ER, vomiting blood.

Leo rubbed his eyes and tried to focus on the activity around him. The heavy, deep bass in the 'by-invitation-only' Vegas nightclub reverberated through his chest.

The DJ expertly dropped the next tune, shaking the walls of the establishment. The music, so loud and so powerful that he felt as if he was in the ocean, deep under, surrounded not by water, but by sound waves, dancers, cocktail waitresses, and clipped conversations. The scent of exclusive perfumes, alcohol, and perspiration spiked the air. This was not new. This had become his escape even before the first time he'd come into money.

He'd been nineteen when the Silicon Valley billionaire Aram Dersch invested in his little idea to the tune of ten million dollars. There was no point in staying in school. He had his ticket to financial independence. Now, nine years later, his solution to everything—from heartbreak to joy—was still alcohol, nightclubs, and new faces. And just like ten years ago, he was still not sure what he was after.

Leo tried to stand, but his body did not respond to his attempt. Seated deep in the very comfortable and very plush sofa of the cordoned V.I.P. area, he knew and appreciated the game the establishment was playing. Keep the patron happy with five thousand dollar bottles of champagne and very attractive and attentive women. But there was one thing they couldn't do—relieve him of the need to visit the restroom.

"Chris," he slurred.

But Chris didn't hear him. When Chris was drunk, he was even more animated than normal. He was talking to a blue-eyed brunette about artificial intelligence and fuzzy logic, and its potential in transforming everything. To her credit, she pretended to be amused by this revelation. Leo wondered if she even spoke English.

He turned to Anna. As always, solid and sober. And as always, watching Leo with the look of concern that he'd come to both appreciate and hate, all at the same time.

"Bathroom?" she asked.

He nodded.

She rose and offered him her hand. "C'mon."

She helped him up and nodded to their security detail to walk with them.

"I really really appreciate you," Leo said as they stumbled toward the restrooms.

She didn't respond.

"And I know you'll lecture me tomorrow," he said, then sighed. "And by the time you're done, I'll resent you." He focused on the placement of his feet. "But for right now, I really appreciate you."

They reached the restroom door. One of the security men held him up.

"It's not there, you know," she said.

"What? What're you talkin' about?"

"Whatever you're looking for. It's not at the bottom of the bottle or in the empty conversation with the next up-and-coming model."

He smiled. "Maybe not. But it's fun trying to find it." He chuckled.

"Remind me how much fun you're really having *after* you kneel in front of the porcelain god and vomit out over a hundred grand of alcohol and caviar."

Twenty minutes later, Leo stumbled out, his shirt partially untucked, but a bit more sure-footed. Night club restrooms were always decked out to address all necessities. The mouth wash was just what this particular occasion called for.

Anna slid her phone in her pocket, then stepped up to him and fixed his collar and pointed to his shirt. "Fix that."

He shoved his hand in and made himself more presentable. He was a known face. Pictures of him showed up on sites all the time. The paparazzi loved him and his parties. And now, with the sale of Vitruvian, more press would hound him. "What time is the press conference?" he asked. They'd flown in from their Silicon Valley offices to Vegas specifically for the various scheduled interviews and joint press conferences.

"Nine." She glanced at her watch. "In six hours."

"Well, crap. I better get to bed."

"While you were in there... doing your thing... I called the car to come around. Chris will get back separately," she said. "By the way, does the name Roberto Chaparral mean anything to you?"

He hesitated. He wanted to say no, but his mind wasn't all there. "Not sure, Anna. Is he from the Valley?"

"Don't think so, but then again, his message is garbled. But I thought he may be an uncle or family."

Leo straightened. He had no family. Other than his father, and he barely counted. "No. No one like that. Why would you think he's family?"

"He called you Lionel in the message. Only those who've known you since before you were you know you by that name."

He proceeded toward the exit. The sound of the entire nightclub disappeared. *Chaparral? Lionel?*

The name Chaparral still didn't ring a bell. But Lionel... yeah, that meant something.

Chapter Three

Catalina

Cat rubbed her eyes as she made her way toward the cafeteria. This place was not her first choice, but it was the only realistic choice. The smell of old, mold, and stale was the signature mark of this establishment. The woman behind the cash register paid her no attention. Her focus was on the overhead T.V. instead. That suited Cat just fine. She wanted a cup of three-hour-old coffee and maybe even a donut. Not a conversation.

She grabbed a large cup and splattered some tar-textured French Roast in it. It smelled prehistoric, but someone once told her that old coffee was more potent. She hoped there was some truth to that because Cat needed the super leaded deal in her veins. The last four, or was it five days, had been particularly hard—both physically and emotionally. She added sugar and some dry creamer until the color looked right. She stirred it, evaluated the color, then added a bit more powder.

There, she thought. She didn't have control over most things in her life. So anytime she could get things just her way was an absolute win in her book.

She went to the donut station, salivated over the chocolate glaze, but hesitated. It was not the sugar or the calories. She was healthy and mostly toned. Splurging with a bit of sugary and fatty food would not harm her. No, her issue was not about health, but about cash.

Cat dug into her purse and pulled out the wallet. She counted the singles and the loose coin. She could afford it. But really, she couldn't.

She pulled out one dollar in change and walked up to the register.

The woman was not even aware of Cat's presence. In the grander scheme of things, Cat was not important. Sadly, for some in this town, she was infamous. For this woman, however, Cat was invisible. Whatever was on the T.V. was clearly more important.

Cat glanced up and froze.

A face from years ago smiled and charmed the host on the cable business network show. The volume was so low that his voice was barely perceptible.

Good. She did not want to hear his voice. She didn't want to know anything about him. Nothing. The banner beneath him declared, "Leo Moncrieff, Vitruvian CEO sells to Gaming Kings."

Cat peeled her eyes away, then cleared her throat.

The woman spun, "Oh, sorry. Didn't see you."

Cat smiled. "No worries."

"Just the coffee?"

"Yeah," she said and handed her the change.

"Ya know, he's originally from here," the woman said, flicking her eyes toward the T.V.

"That right?"

"Yup. Sold his company for billions."

Cat's jaw clenched. "Good for him," Cat said as she sipped her coffee. "Thanks again." She walked away just as the volume increased.

"What's next for you?" the interviewer asked him.

"Celebrate. Pinch myself. Do it all over again."

They laughed. How humorous and charming. And nauseating.

Cat closed her eyes for a moment and visualized spinning around and launching the cup of coffee directly at the screen. But she needed the coffee.

She stepped outside and walked toward her destination. How ironic, she thought. There he was in some studio dazzling the host, flashing his manicured teeth, perfectly styled hair, and chiseled jawline, talking about celebrating, completely unaware and uncaring of what was going on here in the town with the people he had abandoned.

From her purse, she pulled out her key chain. Hanging from it was a memory. A reminder. The ring he'd given her. She ran her thumb over it, then dropped it back in her purse.

Yeah, Leo, you go ahead and pinch yourself, she thought. *You are livin' the dream. Me, I'm survivin' and fightin' the best I can.*

Chapter Four

Leo

"That's a wrap," the production manager called out. "Thank you, Mr. Moncrieff. Let me take the mic off you."

Leo breathed a sigh of relief. A press conference, three interviews, and now he was done. And no one even realized he was still plastered. No one other than Annabelle, who had a sour look on her face.

He shook hands with the interviewer and a couple of other people, then joined Anna as they marched toward the exits.

"You don't have to still look so pissy, Anna. We did it. The interviews are done, and now I can rest for a couple of days."

She shook her head. "It's not that," she said as they stepped outside under the blazing Nevada sun. Their car was waiting for them.

"Then what?" he asked as she slid in, and he followed her.

"Last night—I guess it was this morning—I asked you about a Chaparral."

He straightened. He'd nearly forgotten about that. Sometimes the conversations got lost in the drinks. "Yeah, that's right. Still don't know who he is."

"Well, I do." She bit the inside of her cheek. That was her tell. She wanted to protect him from something.

"Go on, who is he, and what does he want?"

She breathed in and bore into his eyes. "He is your father's attorney. Your dad, Lionel senior, is apparently very ill."

Leo did not blink. Seconds ticked away until he finally said, "And...?"

"Mr. Chaparral wanted you to know that it's not looking good for your dad."

Leo broke eye contact and stared out the window.

Annabelle placed her hand on his shoulder. "Leo? Are you okay?"

He turned to face her. "If Chaparral calls again, thank him for letting me know. Beyond that, I have nothing further to say."

Anna flinched. "Seriously?"

"Seriously."

He turned his attention back to the buildings. Maybe resting was not the best plan. Maybe he needed to get himself invited to a good party tonight.

After much debate, Chris and Anna won. They spent the last night in Las Vegas at the renowned SW Steakhouse at the Wynn Casino. Leo wanted to go to STK, but Anna and Chris overruled him. He liked STK because that steakhouse was more nightclub than a restaurant. The DJ's volume of choice was jet-engine loud, which meant that Leo could avoid conversations. At SW, they would force him to talk. As it happened, they talked about the details of the acquisition, the upcoming World Cup, and even discussed the weather.

Yes, the weather.

"Leo," Chris finally spoke up, "what's going on, man? You gotta let us in. At the risk of sounding completely arrogant, we are the closest friends you have."

Leo studied his friend's face.

"You never talk about your parents," Anna said. "You never talk about where you came from. Almost like you prefer not having a past."

Leo nodded at Anna's observation. He leaned back and picked up his glass of red. "That's because, for all intents and purposes, I have no family left."

"But..." Anna started.

"But I have a father who's not well, right?" Leo finished for her. He took a big swallow, nearly finishing the cup that was meant to be savored, not tossed back. "Sure, he partnered with my mom and they produced me. But he was never more than that on paper. He never liked me."

"Dude..." Chris said.

"Go on," Anna said.

Leo focused in on her. "I was invisible to him. Plain and simple. And when my mom died, he made it very clear that I was better off away from him."

"You're kidding," she said.

What did Anna want to hear? That Leo's dad had called him a loser and that he would never amount to anything, or that he was useless? No, Leo preferred dealing with those demons by himself.

"As far as I'm concerned, I was raised by a single mom. And when she died, I made a promise that I'd make something of myself. So I did what I had to do and have buried the past. All of it. My father, my hometown, and even the girl I gave my ring."

"Ah, yes. The infamous Cat saga," Anna said.

"Bro, I didn't know you were engaged to her," Chris said.

Leo chuckled. "Not exactly engaged." He adjusted himself in the seat. "I gave her my only gold ring as a promise."

"Not a very good promise," he said.

Anna punched his shoulder.

"What?" Chris said, completely oblivious to his lack of tact.

But that's what he appreciated about these two. The man spoke the truth. Had Leo implied together forever? Maybe. *Poor Catalina.* He could still remember how her greenish-brown eyes had become red rimmed in the instant he broke the news. Some decisions could suck in perpetuity.

They were all silent for a few moments. "Where was home again?" Chris asked.

Leo sighed. "A little map dot a few hours south of San Jose called Fortuny Bay."

"Beach town, right?" Chris asked.

"I wish. It was a fishing harbor primarily. It could've been a beach town also, but they never focused on the beaches. The beaches are for bums, the harbor is for real men. Not sure if that was the official motto, but it sure was preached regularly. Fortuny Bay is one of those places that should be an amazing destination for tourists, but there's a cloud over it. Like a murkiness that kept that town from ever becoming anything but a pit stop."

Chris looked up from his phone. "Wow, the topography seems perfect. Good surf?"

"Amazing surf. Hard stuff. But again, it's not on any surfer's destination guide. A couple of hours south, Pismo. A couple of hours north, Santa Cruz."

"Can we get back to the issue at hand?" Anna asked. "Look, it's none of my business—"

"True," Leo said, then grinned. "But you're about to get into my business anyway, right?"

"Well, of course. Could you expect anything less from me?" She adjusted her seat and leaned forward. "I don't know what your dad said or did to you. What I do know is that not forgiving sucks."

"I am *not* forgiving him," Leo said without hesitation.

"Hear me out. Not forgiving him will only hurt and haunt *you*. Particularly since he's not well. He will pass on. Maybe not now, but eventually, we all do. And what you'll be left with is anger and bitterness. He has taken permanent residence in your head and heart. You need to find a way to evict him. Otherwise, he will be there forever."

"Man, she's even a freakin' philosopher," Chris said.

"I'm so tempted to smack you upside the head," Anna said. "Leo, you are militant about completion. You tell the dev teams to bring it home, land the plane, get it done. Cheesy, yes. But you understand what's not closed lingers."

Without breaking eye contact, he tipped his glass and finished the drink.

"Trust me, Leo," she said. "Go there. Speak what you must and clear him from your head."

Chapter Five

Catalina

Cat heard Lola's tires crunch over the gravel driveway. She grabbed her purse and hung it across her body. She downed the cup of coffee, placed the cup in the sink, and ate the last piece of toast.

She sped toward the kitchen door and grabbed the handle just as Lola Morris stepped on the creaky deck. One of these days, someone was going to get hurt when the planks gave way.

She turned the handle and saw Lola's always-beaming face. Neither her beautiful smile nor her gigantic eyes had changed since they'd met in kindergarten. Thankfully, nowadays, Lola's hair style was tight, professionally done braids. Back in the early days, her hair was lovingly called "the mess on my head."

There was nothing messy about her now. She was a loving friend, a dedicated teacher, and had a heart for others that was nearly unreal.

"Thank you so much, Lola," she said and hugged her friend.

"Don't even mention it, sweetie. Any news from the convalescent home?" Lola asked.

"No, thankfully."

"No news is good news, right?"

Cat nodded, then took a deep breath. "It's horrible to say, but I am exhausted."

"It's not horrible. You've been there watching someone who's been like a father to you deteriorate. You are physically and emotionally spent."

She breathed out. "I am," Cat said and dropped her eyes to her feet. "I hate seeing him like this. Weak. Thin."

They both became silent, neither willing to say more.

"Go on, get out of here," Lola said. "Anything I need to know?"

"No. Same drill as always."

"You got it." Lola pulled Cat into a hug. They stayed like that for a few moments until Cat pulled away.

"Thanks for everything."

"Don't mention it again, otherwise you'll have to play me one on one on the blacktop."

Cat smiled. Oh, how they loved to play basketball when they were younger. Lola never learned how to defend Cat's fadeaway jumper.

"One of these days, I'll give you one more chance to lose," Cat said.

Lola's eyes narrowed. "I'm gonna practice. I will get my revenge from all those high school days."

Cat grinned. "We'll see." She dug her hand in her purse for her keys. "Where'd I put the keys?"

"Over here," Lola said as she grabbed them off the kitchen counter. But before she handed them to Cat, she hesitated and studied the key chain. "Still have the ring?"

Cat grabbed the set, unable to make eye contact. "Yeah."

"Thought you were gonna pawn it," Lola said.

"Yeah, was gonna do it but turned out I didn't need the money after all."

Silence.

"Got it," Lola said. Although her words didn't say it, her voice made it clear that she didn't buy Cat's story.

"Anyway, I better go," Cat said.

"Taking the truck?"

"No, the bike. I need a bit of cardio. I feel like I'm falling apart."

Lola nodded. "Be safe."

"Always."

Cat strode out, walked up to her rusty bike, and hopped on. She kicked off and rode down the road to the convalescent home.

Thought you were gonna pawn it.

Sometimes she wished Lola wasn't so observant, or so aware of all the details in her life. But if not her, then who? She had no one.

Poor Lionel had been so sick for so long that she wouldn't even think about bringing up things like that. So it had to be Lola. Only Lola.

Unfortunately, she'd lied to her best friend. Truth is that she could always use the money. And even though Lionel always offered her money, she would accept nothing that didn't have to do with necessities. She didn't want him to know how deep of a hole she was in.

She didn't need help. She'd figure it out... somehow. She always found a way. No matter how dark or painful things got, God always opened a door for her. That's all she needed—faith and a bit of luck.

As for the ring. She should've gotten rid of it a decade ago. She should've tossed it, given it away, or sold it. But try as she might, she just could never get herself to do it.

Not because she wanted to hold on to his promises. The ring was not about him. But because those days held the possibility of a beautiful life. That was the first time she remembered feeling fulfilled. The ring represented a time in her life that she was complete and whole. And she held on to the belief that she'd one day have that again.

Somehow.

Someday.

Chapter Six

Leo

Leo arrived home early the next morning. As much as he liked the vibe of San Francisco, he didn't want to live there. That beautiful city had been turning weird and a bit too eccentric for him. He also felt insulted when he was told the 1,300 square foot apartment with the "splendid view" was a steal at five million. He was a lot happier in the San Jose slash Stanford area. Close to the city, much better pricing—relatively speaking—and closer to nature.

You are a small-town boy, he recalled his father saying once. He gritted his teeth. Just for that, he decided he would buy another penthouse in London.

He shook his head as he reached his front door, which automatically unlocked and the double doors opened. Leo loved technology. He left his luggage at the entrance and tossed his jacket on the kitchen counter. He needed a drink. Maybe many drinks.

He'd been very happy. He was at the peak of his career. But now, he wasn't feeling the joy. He had left the past in the past. That's what he had learned. Leave it there and move on. So why did it feel like the *past* was sitting on the face of the *present* and not allowing the *future* to breathe?

Instead of a drink, he decided a few laps in his pool were what he really needed. He quickly changed into trunks and went into his backyard. From his phone, he played what sounded like a club mix but was, in fact, a workout tempo mix. The entire backyard came to life with music blaring from dozens of speakers. He even had specialized speakers installed inside the pool focused on the bass so that he could feel the music in the water. Yeah, it was stupid, but it sounded like a brilliant idea at the time.

Did you put on the sunscreen?

Even now, he could hear his mom's voice. No, he hadn't put on sunscreen. He used to reason that his olive complexion was natural protection. And although there may have been some truth to that since his mom's side were fifth-generation Spaniards—he also didn't want to tempt fate. He lathered some on, then jumped in the water.

The water was perfectly heated. His entire body relaxed as he effortlessly swam one lap after another. All the noise in his head disappeared and what remained was his breathing and the undeniable beat that set the tempo for his strokes.

At the end of the fortieth lap, he stopped. He normally went for sixty before stopping, but today he was not all there. He hopped out, splashed toward the refrigerator and pulled out an ice-cold beer. Maybe he'd invite Anna and Chris over. Another party before Chris disappeared for three months as part of the transition agreement with Gaming Kings. Those two were the only people he trusted. Truth be told, he would not allow anyone to speak to him with that level of candor. But he knew those two cared for him with no ulterior motives.

He drained the beer. Why had his father's lawyer really reached out? His father no doubt had self-serving motives. Had he heard about the deal and now wanted to befriend his long-lost son? So cliché. He'd pretend he was sick just to get his super-wealthy estranged son to show up. He wasn't even that old, so what could possibly be wrong. Hemorrhoids?

How sad that he couldn't even trust his own father. But anyone who'd been there would understand him. His father was and always would be an unhappy man who never deserved the wife he had. Leo's mom, on the other hand, was an angel. Why she married him, he'd never know. That question had not been high on his fifteen-year-old mind when she passed away more than a decade ago.

In that moment, he recalled a snippet from one of the many conversations he had with her on her last days.

He'll need you. He has no one else.

Is that what she told him? He thought about it and even saw her pale face, and her chapped lips say those words.

No. He would not fall through that rabbit hole. After all these years, it was best that they kept their distance. Leo was certain that if they came face to face, they'd both say things they'd regret.

But what if he really was sick? And what if his father didn't know about what Leo had accomplished?

He has no one else.

By going, by showing up, would Leo be able to let go of all that resentment he'd held on to? Maybe he'd even get off his chest something he wanted to say for all these years. Unlike his last attempt at telling him off—just the memory of that failed attempt two years earlier made him cringe—this time, he could have an adult conversation.

He'll need you.

Why now? Why did he have to remember her words? What would Leo say? What would either say? Would there be any mutual ground? Everything Leo had ever done was wrong or done poorly. There was only one thing he'd done well, according to his father. And of course, he had left her when he escaped the small world for the big one.

Not forgiving him will only hurt and haunt you.

That's what Anna had said. The moment she spoke the words, he knew she was right.

Now he had both his mom and Anna speaking into his head. There was no winning this one. He'd regret it either way. But maybe it was time. If not now, then when?

Leo rushed back into his house, grabbed his luggage, and rolled it to his room. Once there, he unzipped the bag, turned it upside down, dropping everything inside into a pile on the floor. He pulled a couple of drawers open and pulled out clean clothes, and placed those inside the empty luggage.

What are you doing, Leo?

He wasn't sure. But as he slid into the shower, he felt a sense of urgency. Like this was the time to surface everything and be done with it.

He changed, grabbed his bag and other essentials, and considered the car options. He would not take the Ferrari there, nor the Maserati. The classic Sting Ray was for special occasions only. That left only one other option. He jumped into the gift that Elon Musk had personally given Leo. His custom Cybertruck. When he put down the address, his Tesla pointed out that there were no charging stations in Fortuny Bay. There were some just outside of town.

They barely have electricity there, he thought, and grinned.

A new idea dawned on him. He jumped out and rolled the camping kit into the Cybertruck's bed. Maybe he'd go camping once he spoke with his father. It was time he tested this beast out.

He pulled out his mobile and texted Anna.

> Going to Fortuny Bay

Ten seconds later, she replied.

> I prayed you would. Even my mom prayed for you.

Leo grinned. Had she actually asked her mom in Nashville to pray for him? He thought that was sort of cool, even though he put little stock in positive thoughts and good energy.

Another message popped up from her.

What about security? she wrote.

He considered for a second then replied, *It's a sleepy town. Nothing's gonna happen.*

When he thought she was done, another message popped up. *You want me to come with?*

He paused and seriously considered it. *Nah*, he wrote. *I'll only be there for a few hours.*

If you say so, she replied.

As he pulled out of his garage, he wondered what she meant or what she knew. She always made ominous statements like that, and sometimes her words echoed true.

If you say so...

"Yes, I do," he said out loud and drove off.

Chapter Seven

Catalina

C at waved at the receptionist and marched toward Lionel's room. She moderated her breathing. The bike ride had been good for her. Her lungs were actually laboring a bit. She needed more of that.

She gently knocked on the door and entered Lionel's room.

"Good morning," she said as she carefully tread in.

Lionel's eyes were half closed. But when he heard her voice, he turned his head toward her. A faint smile parted his lips.

"Top o' the mornin' to you," he said.

"Top o' the mornin' right back at you." It broke her heart to hear his feeble voice. "Want some water?"

He nodded.

She grabbed the pink plastic cup, poured fresh water, and plopped the straw inside it before she brought it to his lips. He tried to hold the cup. "I got it, Lionel. You just drink."

He did. Only a few sips. He was getting weaker. But she didn't want to think of that. She didn't want to accept the doctor's predictions. They'd been wrong about everything so far. Why not this?

He put up his thumb. His way of saying he was good.

She put the cup on his little side table.

"How's Francisco?" he asked.

"Everyone's fine. We're just waiting for you to get better."

He chuckled. "Sure. Why not?" His face suddenly got serious, and he faced her. "I'm not gonna let them win."

"Stop thinking about that stuff. Focus on getting out of here."

His face got a fresh surge of color. "That's all that matters. Winning. And you better keep your eyes wide open. Very few people that can be trusted."

He was right about that. Everyone had an agenda. "Thankfully, there are some good folk here," she said.

He grunted. "Can count them on one hand. Me and you included."

She laughed. "There's Lola."

He nodded. "She's a good egg."

Her spirit lifted. He seemed to have a renewed source of energy. Maybe he was getting better. "There's your friend Chaparral."

He spun to her. "He's a lawyer," he said.

"He's also your friend."

"He's a lawyer," he repeated. "They don't have friends."

She laughed. "Okay, but not all lawyers are bad."

For the first time in days, she saw him laugh.

"Oh, Catalina," he said as he tried to catch his breath. "You are a good person. Naïve, but good."

"Did you just call me naïve?" she asked, pretending like she was insulted.

He glanced at her. "Yes. But I also said good."

She fake glared at him. "Okay, I'll give you a pass on that one."

He grinned, seemingly impressed at his ability to get himself out of a tight situation. He sank his head into the pillow and closed his eyes.

"Are you okay?" she asked.

"Living the dream. Just tired," he said. "So tired."

She placed her hand on his.

"Tired of this place," he said, his eyes remained closed. "Tired of the doctor. The nurses. The limited T.V. channels. The bland food. The conversations. Decisions. Just tired of… everything."

She waited him out.

"Wanna play cards?" she asked.

"Nah, you'll cheat." He smiled, even though his eyes remained closed.

Her jaw dropped. "When have I cheated?"

But he didn't respond. He just continued to smile.

"Lionel?" she asked as she squeezed his hand. She glanced at the monitor. His heartbeat looked fine. And his chest rose and lowered. He seemed fine.

Just then, an alarm went off.

[illegible]

Chapter Eight

Leo

Leo had been on Pacific Coast Highway for just over an hour when he reached Monterey. He pulled over to get a bite at a small mom and pop shop. This family sure knew what they were doing with the fresh catch.

After he got his sandwich and clam chowder in a sourdough bowl, he sat on the truck's tailgate and watched the ocean. It was a bit cold, and the winds that picked up the spray of the crashing waves made the air and everything in the vicinity damp. Man, he missed the ocean. He didn't do this often enough. He used to love camping and hiking and surfing, but in the last decade, there were more planes and conference rooms than lakes and streams.

This was a rare opportunity for him to rest, recover, and recenter himself. He had new business ideas, but he needed a break before he launched the next startup.

His phone rang from inside the Cybertruck. He left the food on the tail of the truck, then ran inside the cabin. It was Anna.

"Hey, you read my mind," he said. "I need the lawyer's contact info. I assume my father's at the clinic or hospice center, since the nearest hospital is a good thirty miles outside of town. Also—"

"Leo, I just spoke to Mr. Chaparral...."

A momentary hesitation.

"What happened?" he asked.

"I'm so sorry, Leo. Your dad passed away."

The sound of crashing waves enveloped him.

"I am so sorry," she repeated.

A few seconds drifted by.

"Send me the info," he said.

"I'm gonna find you a place to stay. I can be there by tomorrow morning," she said.

"No need for you to come."

"You'll need to make arrangements. There are a lot of details to process."

He sighed. "I'll let you know if I need help."

"Where will you stay?" Anna asked.

"If I need to stay, I guess I can stay at my... my mom's home."

She said a few more things, but he wasn't listening. After they hung up, Leo remained in his car for a few minutes. No thoughts. No specific memories. He just sat there, frozen.

He suddenly heard the barking of seagulls and saw a bunch of birds in his rearview mirror fighting over his food.

By the time he got out, they were gone and so was his food. He locked up the rear, threw away the trash in the nearby bin, and slid back in behind the wheel.

He studied the address that Anna texted him. It was the convalescent center. He transferred it to navigation system and allowed the car to drive him there. He did not trust himself right now.

He sank into the plush seat and stared outside the passenger side window. After nearly a decade of not thinking about his father, in a matter of less than 48 hours, Leo was thrown an unexpected curveball.

His father was, at most, in his mid-sixties. Yes, that was not young, but honestly, that was far from old. What did he have? A heart attack? Cancer? He'd find out soon enough.

Now what? Go to the convalescent and sign papers? Presumably a burial or cremation. Did he have a will? Would his lawyer know what he wanted?

Tears ran down his face. He immediately wiped them with his palm and crossed his arms. Why was he crying? That man had been nothing but bad to Leo. Leo successfully kept himself at a safe distance because he didn't want to have anything to do with him. Leo slammed the dashboard. Why did he have to get involved? Why had he even decided to head back to Fortuny Bay?

So much he had wanted to say. So much that would never get aired out.

He saw the sign up ahead, 'Welcome to Fortuny Bay.'

When he was younger, he was told that Fortuny was Italian for fortune. The legend was that the original settlers found tremendous fortune with early commercial fishing. What fortunes awaited the people who lived here now? Nothing, unless they wanted to maintain the harbor or be the skipper of the next rockfish ship or be the next sardine king of the season.

That's why he left. He needed opportunity. He needed a place to explore and grow. He had goals, expectations. And this place not only did it not motivate kids to grow and explore, it, in fact, showed them that there was nothing out there for their kind. From kindergarten to high school, the fishery life was pounded into their heads. Even though it had beautiful beaches, what mattered was commercial fishing. That was it.

What this town represented to someone like Leo was death. A death to dreams. A death to aspirations. And now, for Leo, Fortuny Bay would forever be the place for him to visit the dead.

He took over the car's controls and drove through town first. Fortuny Bay wasn't a small town, but it was a sedate town. The downtown area was small but had all the amenities a town should have. A decent-sized clinic, a couple of dentists, and so on. For a town of just over four thousand people, it was appropriate. On the oceanfront, the southmost edge was the harbor and the docks, and as you traveled further north, the beaches took over.

But for as long as Leo could remember, the city council was stuck in the past and only cared about all things fishing. They would not allow permits to bring new things in, or to renovate, or to modernize. Not Amish, but definitely not forward-minded.

Wasn't always like this, his father used to say. But he only had negative things to say about all politicians. In general, his father was not part of the "In" crowd. For one, he was not of Spanish descent. He was a 'Franchute' as the people in town would say, which was a derogatory way of saying he was of French descent. And although Leo's mom was of Spanish descent—like the majority of town—Leo was considered mixed. Leo had decked his share of kids for calling him that.

How stupid and childish that adults drew boundary lines by their bloodlines. Five generations of Spaniards believed their blood made them the true natives. He was certain some indigenous people held differing opinions.

He crisscrossed the streets and noticed that many of the locals were staring at him. Check that—they were staring at his truck. A red Ferrari would've possibly gotten more looks, but the enormity and futuristic look of the truck was clearly something that most hadn't seen before.

Guess I can't hide out for too long.

He checked the storefronts, recognizing some. He also noted that the name 'Roca' was plastered everywhere. From a couple of banks to a realtor, to a library, school, and even a park. He did not remember seeing that name on the buildings a decade ago. And yet, the name sounded familiar. How and who, he could not put his finger on it.

He went to his childhood home next. His car remained idle in front of the house that, when he was younger, seemed so much bigger and well kept.

Casa Moncrieff used to be a place of prominence in this town. A beacon of sorts that held the highest elevation in town. It perched over the town, like a patron saint, as his mom used to say. On the rear side, the house watched the ocean—the western front—and what marked the approximate end of the sandy beaches. On the front side, the eastern view was a perfect panoramic of the entire town.

This house used to be the focal point of town. At one time, they even had a plaque with *Casa Moncrieff* on it. What most didn't know was that originally the plaque just said *Casa*. Not because it was a house. That was his mother's maiden name. When she married his father, they added his last name. Two families, one iconic home. Or at least it was. But now, the paint was peeling. The wood shingles were rotted or falling apart. The windows were one storm away from becoming open breezeways. The grass... was non-existent. Instead, it was all dirt and gravel now.

For a moment, everything changed. The house was perfect. The grass lush and on the front porch stood his mom, in a bright sundress, waving at him. Her ever-present radiant smile shone and hanging from her shoulder, her art bag. She always drew, painted, colored and imagined.

The past disappeared.

How he wished she were still alive.

He took a deep breath and turned his attention to the side of the house. Parked to the side was his father's rusty old truck. The truck that, for a couple of years, had been Leo's truck.

A fist bore into his gut, then twisted and turned. Cat and Leo shared a lot of memories in that truck. He even told her he loved her in the truck's bed. He had meant it. Now he wondered if he even knew what it meant to utter those words. When he left her, those words, that sentiment, stayed here in Fortuny Bay. And as is with all things in this place, those words and their meaning died here, too.

Chapter Nine

Leo

Leo drove up to the convalescent home. He double-checked the name of the facility against Anna's text. He was wasting time; he knew that. The GPS would not make a mistake. But maybe he was making a mistake by just being here. He felt like a fraud. He didn't know his father and didn't love his father and wouldn't miss his father. And yet, here he was. Why then?

For Mom, he convinced himself.

He hopped out of his truck, walked through the double doors, and asked the information booth for directions to his father's room.

"Can I ask who you are?" the woman asked.

He hesitated. "Lionel Moncrieff junior. I'm his son."

Her eyes went wide. "My, I didn't realize he had a son."

Leo was tempted to say, "My father didn't realize that either." But he just offered her a smile.

"My condolences. Mr. Moncrieff's room is number 27." She lowered her voice. "We have contacted the mortuary."

"Thank you," he said, and walked toward the room.

He stepped in, and memories of his mom in a similar room rushed back into his heart. He was young back then. Not prepared for loss and the implications of being alone. Now, he was older, and the man who lay there was practically a stranger.

He hesitantly moved in, looked at his father, and breathed out. He was thin. So thin that for a second, Leo thought this wasn't his father. But he was. All else remained as Leo remembered. The man had been bald for most of his life, and gray had set in when Leo was in elementary school. His father looked so peaceful. His mouth partially open, his eyes closed, and his skin pale.

Leo never wanted to dislike his father. But his father never liked Leo. Never hugged him, never said a word of encouragement, or expressed any affection toward him. They were acquaintances at best. So why did Leo feel a complete and total emptiness enter his soul as he looked at his father's lifeless body?

Opportunity lost, he heard in his head. He frowned. He wasn't convinced that was really what he believed.

You are alone, he heard. He was. He had no other family... that he knew of.

He slumped into the chair that was placed right next to his father's still body.

"Sorry I was late," Leo whispered. "I'd always hoped that maybe—"

"Can I help you?" a woman from behind him asked.

He rose and turned. "I'm..." but he could not finish the sentence.

Standing in front of him was Catalina. The woman who had been his girlfriend throughout all of high school. The woman he promised he'd marry. The woman he left brokenhearted and alone.

Her long auburn hair was now shorter, just below her shoulder. Her hazel eyes still held the same amount of green. Her sun-touched skin had lost some of its bronze but still glowed. She looked amazing. Older, stronger. Angrier.

"Cat?" he asked. "What are you—?"

Her red-rimmed eyes narrowed. "Now you come, Leo? Now that he's dead?"

He flinched. "Wait. What?"

"Your father had been sick for three years. Three! And now you show up in your designer shoes and fitted pants."

He dropped his eyes and studied his pants. *What the—?* He snapped back up to her. "Well, it's nice to see you, too, Cat. How am I doin', you ask? I'm well, thanks for asking."

"I don't care how you're doing. Why would I care?" Her eyes turned blood red. "This man..." but she did not finish her sentence. The tears streamed down her cheeks uncontrollably. She just stared at him, clenching her jaw.

"Cat..." he started, but she stopped him.

"He didn't deserve to go this way," she breathed out.

A knock on the door. They both turned toward the entrance.

"You must be Lionel," the man said and offered a hand. "My condolences, Son. I'm Roberto Chaparral, your dad's friend and attorney." They shook hands. He then turned to Cat, and they hugged for a few moments. "He's free now," he said to her.

Free of what wondered Leo. But he felt that this was not the time to admit further ignorance.

Chaparral turned to Leo while he still draped one arm over her shoulder. "I ask, out of respect, that you two put the anger and hurt away until after Lionel has been put to rest. He's gone now, and you two are his family."

Leo blinked. How was she family, exactly? Yet another question that he'd have to hold off for now.

"I can take care of everything," she said, then turned to Leo. "You don't have to stay. I know you're busy." The sarcasm owned its own zip code.

As angry as he wanted to be with her for attacking him and judging him, once he stared into her eyes, he couldn't help but feel some level of empathy for her. Clearly, she was distraught. His father's death had hit her hard.

"I want to stay," he said. "I *will* stay."

She offered a curt nod.

"Thank you, both," Chaparral said. "Now, if you'll excuse me, I need to talk to the mortuary."

"What can I do?" she asked Roberto.

"Nothing. Everything is handled for the most part. You'll have other things to tend to."

She nodded.

Leo extended a hand. "Thank you for contacting me," he said.

"It wasn't easy to get through your people, but I am glad we reached you."

They shook, and he left the room.

Cat and Leo looked at each other.

"It's good to see you, Cat."

Her eyes narrowed for a second. She breathed in and out. "I so want to yell at you right now. So many things that are rushing at me. I mean... after all these years... I'm so tempted to punch you."

"I'd block it."

Her jaw dropped open. After a few comebacks attempted to form on her lips but failed to produce a sound, she shook her head. "How do you do that?"

"How do I do what?"

"Walk in here and make it seem like all's good, and we're all just friends. Let's go sing at a karaoke bar."

He thought about it for a second. "Fortuny Bay has a karaoke bar?"

She sighed, then maneuvered around him up to Leo's dad. She ran a gentle hand across his forehead and said, "God bless you, Lionel. Rest In Peace. You're with Cèlia now."

Leo stared at her like she was an alien. God bless you? Did she really think he was with his mom? And where? Heaven? He didn't know who she thought she was talking to, but there was no way the man that he knew was deserving of those words and sentiments. Leo needed clarity, and soon. This time, without coming across as a complete jerk.

She faced him. "Let's go somewhere else and talk," she said.

She didn't have to ask twice.

Chapter Ten

Catalina

Cat marched out of the clinic, not bothering to check to see if his greatness, King Leo, was following her. Why did he come? Why did Chaparral call him? It was practically a blessing that Lionel passed away without seeing Leo.

That's wrong. Stop it. I shouldn't have thought that.

But on some level, it was true. Leo would've come with his superior, I am better than y'all attitude. Excuse me, 'better than you' attitude. She chuckled.

"What's funny?" he asked as he matched her speed and walked alongside her.

"Nothing," she mumbled.

They walked in perfect timing. They used to walk this town together all the time. They even held hands. On those hot summer days, their hands would get all sweaty, but neither wanted to be the one to pull away. He used to joke, "We're stuck together."

"Where to?" he asked.

49

"The diner," she said and pointed toward the pale blue sign reading *Andy's Burgers and Shakes*.

"Ah, dude. You're kidding me. Andy's is still in business?"

"Not everyone ran away." Oh, that felt so good and so wrong. But she needed to get one in.

He did not reciprocate. Instead, he remained silent. As they reached the door, she felt a bit guilty. It was not like her to be mean and say hurtful things. She looked at his reflection in the glass door. He looked somber. She needed to calm herself. Despite it all, he had just lost his dad.

She walked in, waved to a server, and took a booth. He sat across from her.

As she scanned the menu that she knew better than the manager himself, she found the courage to say what needed to be said. "Sorry about that," she mumbled.

"What?" he asked.

"What I said earlier."

"You said a lot of things earlier."

She seethed as she stared into his eyes. Those smiling golden-brown eyes would not derail her. "You know what I'm talkin' about."

"Oh, you mean that below the belt comment about running away? No need to apologize. I did run away. I don't deny it."

She slid the menu into the side compartment, somewhat surprised by his maturity. "Well, that's refreshing. When we last spoke—"

"Hey sweetie," said the server, Dee, to Cat as she slid two glasses of water. "Who's this fine-dressed young man?" But when she looked directly at his face, her mouth opened wide, and her chewing gum almost dropped out. "Lionel?"

He smiled. "Hey, Dee."

"Get up and give us a hug," she said, and he complied. She wouldn't let go. "It's been so long. Why didn't you visit us?"

Cat coughed and felt Leo's eyes on her.

He pulled away. "Well, I'm here now. How have you been? How's Tony?"

"Shoo, not as good as you," she said and laughed. "Didn't we just see you on the T.V. yesterday or somethin'?"

"Don't know. I try not to watch too much of that. Too much fake news."

"They say you a billionaire."

He coughed. "Definitely fake news."

"Did you come to visit your dad?"

As he sat, Cat interjected. "Hey, Dee... he passed on. Just a bit ago."

Dee placed a hand on Cat's shoulder and squeezed. "He won't suffer no more. A blessing in the bigger scheme of things."

Cat nodded. Still hurt to lose him. But she agreed.

Dee turned to Leo. "My condolences."

He thanked her. Dee took their order, then walked off.

Silence.

"Cat, I need some background. Can you bring me up to speed on what happened with my... my..."

"Your dad?" She couldn't believe it. "You can say it, you know."

He clenched his jaw. "I know I can say it, Cat. Just bring me up to speed on what happened with my father."

She chuckled. "You still can't say it."

"I just did."

"You said father."

He looked at her like she was speaking in Aramaic. "And?" he asked.

"You can't say dad."

He blinked.

"Stumped you, didn't I?"

He grabbed the water and downed half of it. "As much fun as it is to engage in verbal tennis with you, can you put aside all your anger, resentment, and judgment and instead tell me what happened with him?"

She felt like he had just punched her. Was she angry? Resentful? Was she judging him? She rewound her words. Everything she didn't want to be, everything she disliked in others, came out of her when she was with him.

"Sorry," she said. "It's just that you're bringing out the worst in me."

"Umm. Not a very good apology."

She closed her eyes. "Anyway..." she said.

"Look, no need to apologize. Let's just speak, okay?"

She nodded. "Okay."

"You said he'd been sick for three years. With what?"

Their fries and drinks arrived.

"I wish I could tell you. Even to this day, they don't know what caused his issues." She ate a few pieces of fries as he squeezed ketchup and added mustard to it. He mixed the concoction. "It's some sort of blood disorder where he continually lost blood. But they didn't know how he was losing it. Initially, it was about regularly scheduled blood transfusions, which got very expensive because Medicare didn't cover all of it. Then it became painful. If he grabbed something, his skin would turn black."

Leo stopped eating and placed his elbows on the table, and steepled his fingers in front of his mouth. He processed it for a few seconds, then finally spoke. "For three years? They couldn't figure out what was wrong all that time? What about specialists?"

She shook her head. "Your dad didn't have that kind of money. Chaparral encouraged him to take a loan against the house or sell it, but your dad was not about to part with the home or end up owing money when he lived on a fixed income. For him, that was a setup for financial disaster."

Leo shut his eyes, then ran his hands ran over his eyes, across the forehead, and landed on his temples, where he squeezed for a few moments. He sighed.

"What's wrong?" she asked.

He pulled away his hands, revealing red eyes. "Guilt. It's a crappy companion," he said matter-of-factly.

"Oh," she said, and it dawned on her that she'd done exactly what she didn't want to do—make him wonder if he could've possibly saved his father. "You didn't know," she offered.

"No, I didn't." A beat. "Not to be rude, but why are you involved, Cat? What is it I don't know?"

She hesitated. How much was she willing to share with him? He was practically a stranger. Leo had left his family, his friends, and her—the girl he'd given his high school ring to as a promise. He never called or emailed or anything. She went with the obvious answer. "As you may recall, he always liked me."

Leo nodded. "That he did."

She sipped her drink as she recalled those days.

"So over the years, the circumstances lined up, and I became his caretaker."

"Wow," he said. "Did you go into nursing or…"

"No, nothing like that. I helped him in any way I could."

He seemed to process her words. "I guess he didn't lose you after all." He smiled as he ate a piece of fry.

"What do you mean?" she asked.

"On the day I told him I'm leaving, he let me know exactly how he felt. He pointed out my track record of messing up everything I'd touched. He admitted that I'd only done one thing right—you. And by leaving, I messed that up, too. Looks like he was a lot more comfortable losing me than you."

"That's not fair."

"Maybe not, but it is factually accurate." He studied her for a moment. "I'd like to see the house."

"Sure," she said and pulled a couple of crumpled-up bills.

He stopped her. "Please, Cat. I got this."

"I can pay for my own things," she said, knowing full well she really couldn't.

He stopped her. "I owe you much more than just French fries."

Her instinct was to say no, but with the passing of Lionel, she needed to be careful with what little she had. "I also got a shake," she said.

He smiled and placed a very large bill on the table.

She hated him for placing that type of money on the table. And she hated him more for smiling at her.

[illegible]

Chapter Eleven

Leo

When they returned to the clinic, she walked up to the bicycle rack and pulled out her neon green dirt bike. That bike must've been amazing in the 1960s.

"I'll give you a ride," Leo said.

"It's fine."

"Don't get all weird. We'll put that Smithsonian classic in the bed of my truck and drive up."

She seemed surprised. "You have a truck? I thought you would've shown up in a Lambo or something."

He scoffed. "What do you take me for? Lambos are way too overrated." He would not admit that he had one in his place in London.

She rolled her bike next to him as they approached the beast. He pressed a button, and the Cybertruck's covered tail rolled up, exposing the bed.

"This is your idea of a truck?"

He looked at her, then back to the truck. "Yeah, what's the problem?"

"The problem? Well, for one, this is not a truck. It's a DeLorean from Back to the Future on steroids."

Leo was nearly insulted. "This is an amazing piece of machinery." The ramp rolled out automatically. "Give me your bike," he said.

"I can manage. Thank you." She walked the bike up the ramp, then leaned it onto the bed. She hopped down. "Does it give you a neck rub while you drive?"

"Ridiculous," he said. "But it does give a mean foot massage."

She laughed and quickly recovered. Was he winning her over? Maybe.

They drove the three miles in relative silence until they reached the house. He breathed in and picked up her scent. Something tugged his gut. Memories? Guilt? He checked himself and focused on the road.

When he saw the house again, a bit of sadness draped over him. If his mom had seen the house in this state, it would've broken her heart. He drove the truck over the dirt path and parked it next to the large detached garage.

"Forgot to ask if you have the keys to the house," he said as they jumped out and walked toward the house.

She gave him a quizzical look. "Well, of course. I live here."

He stopped. "You what?" he asked, and at the same instant, the side door leading to the kitchen swung open. A little boy, maybe five or six years old, ran out, followed by someone else from his past.

"Mama," the kid said and rammed into her arms. She lifted him and sat him on her hip as she kept walking.

"Thank you, Lola," Cat said.

They hugged, squeezing the boy in between. "I am so sorry, Cat."

"Thank you, but he's better off. We all know that."

Lola nodded and then saw the car and noticed Leo. "Leo?" she asked. Her shock was evident in her wide-open eyes.

Although he'd wiped out all these faces and names from his memory, there was no way Lola would ever be forgotten.

"Hey there," he said as they embraced. For the longest time, they were best of friends. By high school, they were still friendly, just not as close, and after he left… well, he didn't keep in touch with anyone from Fortuny Bay.

As they let go, she took a step back, then punched his shoulder. "Jerk!"

"Hey," he protested as he rubbed his shoulder.

"That's not nice," the boy said.

Leo spun to the voice and leaned down. "Thank you, little man. What's your name?"

"Chicho. But that's just my nickname. I'm five. Is that your spaceship?"

"My name is Leo. That's also my nickname. I'm twenty-eight, and yes, that is indeed my spaceship, but they won't let me fly her. So for now, I just drive her on the streets."

"Don't lie to the kid," Lola said. "How long were you in a Turkish prison?"

He gave her a look. "I was never in a prison."

"Then what's your excuse for not calling any of us?"

"Oh," he said. "That." He hesitated. *Think. Think.* "Love the hair."

"Good save," she said.

"Let's go in, guys," Cat said. "It's hot out here."

"I need to take off," Lola said, "but I expect an explanation next time I see you." She made the motion that she was about to punch him, but then pulled him into another embrace. "You really are a jerk," she whispered.

"I know," he whispered back.

He followed Cat inside while Chicho walked next to him. "Will you give me a ride in your spaceship?"

"If… umm… your mama says yes, then yes."

"Will you, mama? Mama? Ma?"

"Okay, both of you need to stop. Francisco, sweetie, please go inside and play with your Legos or cars while we talk about mister Lionel."

"Lola told me he's in heaven now," Chicho said.

Leo held different opinions on the matter.

"Yes, Sweetie, he's in heaven."

When Chicho was out of earshot, Leo tapped her shoulder. "So, you… you two live here?"

"Yeah. For the last three years."

"And... your husband...?"

She hesitated. Looked deep into his eyes. "I'm a widow. Can we talk about arrangements for your dad's funeral?"

A widow. He must've died around the time she and Francisco moved in here. But why here? He would have to hold on to those questions for now.

They sat at the wobbly kitchen table. He scanned the room. Leo wouldn't say that the place was falling apart. For the most part, of the things he'd seen in the house so far, everything looked the same. Just older. Nothing had been replaced or updated. They were kept up and cleaned, but they were old. The sharp contrast to his life, to what he was used to, was staggering, to say the least. Sitting in this kitchen, on these squeaky chairs, he knew without a doubt that he had indeed run away. From death to life.

However, there was something else that was undeniable. Beneath all the decay, his mom's touch could still be seen and felt. The placement of flower vases. The curtains and small decorations. It was all Cèlia.

"Your dad was very specific," Cat said, pulling him out of his thoughts. "No funeral, no ceremony. He wanted to be cremated."

"Just like Mom," Leo said.

"Yes, and apparently, when your mom passed, he bought two slots, so nothing to buy. The mortuary will cremate him in a few days and then move his remains to the slot."

"Then I guess there isn't much to do," he said.

"Other than the house and his possessions."

They both scanned the room. There was a lot in the house.

"What are your plans?" she asked.

He ran his hand over his stubbles. "Well, I had no plans. Coming here, I assumed I was about to visit him. I don't know if he owes anything on this home."

"He doesn't."

He sighed. "That makes it easier. I don't know. Maybe sell, I guess," he said, but as he said that, something in his gut churned. Could he sell his mom's home?

She dropped her eyes to her hands. "I see."

Did she have a place to stay if he sold this place? Did she even have a job?

"I mean, no rush or anything. You know, with you and your son."

She shook her head. "No, no, that's fine. We'll be okay." But he didn't believe her. "Probably move in with Lola. What I... what you may not know was that the dream had always been to renovate *Casa Moncrieff* to its original glory and make it into a bed-and-breakfast."

Leo was about to say that he didn't particularly care for what his father planned and dreamt of. He'd never been interested in Leo's dreams and plans. Why should he care about his father's?

"Can I look around?" he asked instead, changing the topic.

"Of course." She rose. He took a cursory glance at the large living room and dining room. They headed toward the stairs. "Francisco and I took your mom's sewing room," she said as they stepped up the creaking stairs to the second floor.

"You're sharing a room?" he asked, surprised as they reached the second floor landing. "Why not use one of the many spare rooms or what used to be my room on the third floor?"

"Well, the other rooms became storage areas and your dad was not up to doing any heavy lifting," she said.

He glanced at what would've been his parents' room, but was not ready to see it.

"As for your room..." she trailed. She continued up the stairs to the third floor that only had one room—his. They stopped in front of his room. She opened the door.

He trudged in, then slowly scanned the room, stunned.

"Not one thing was changed in your room after you left," she said.

Literally, everything was as he left it. The printouts that he had no longer needed for his trip. The pen that he used to write the last note to his father. The room felt like a literal time machine. He touched his desk. Not a speck of dust.

"I... I don't understand," he said, his voice a bit hoarse.

"I don't either, if I'm being honest. But he wouldn't let anyone mess with it. When he could no longer do it himself, he asked if I could dust this room regularly."

Leo dropped onto his bed. "But... why? He hated me." He fought against the tears that were threatening the avalanche. Leo would not cry. Not here. Not now.

She sat next to him. "No, Leo. He didn't hate you. I don't know what he felt, but I don't believe he knew how to handle the emotions he felt. He didn't know any better."

Leo rose. He didn't want to hear any of this, and he certainly didn't want to see this. "Look, I better call the office and get an update. There's a lot going on."

She rose, too. "Yeah, of course. I need to prepare food for Chicho, anyway."

She left the room. He scanned it one more time, then marched out and headed to his truck. He needed air. He needed to get out of this house.

Chapter Twelve

Catalina

Cat watched Leo storm out of the house and enter his truck. She didn't want to feel empathy for this guy. He was not a good guy. He had turned his back on everyone. She didn't begrudge him for wanting to have a better life. Who didn't want that? But why cut off everyone? Even those who'd been there for him through it all.

"Help me, Mama," Chicho said as he handed her Lego pieces.

She sat on the floor next to him and separated the pieces that were tightly squeezed together. She needed a bit of solitude. Maybe take a walk on the beach and deal with all the emotions she was feeling right now. She knew Lionel was very ill. She knew he would pass sooner than later. But now he was gone. She no longer had the one person who'd taken a stand for her and her son.

Her phone rang.

She slid it out of her back pocket, read Lola's name, and answered.

"Hey."

"Can you talk, or is he near you?" Lola asked.

"I can talk."

A beat.

"Then talk! What's going on? How did he know? What did he say? What did you say? Spill something already."

Cat swapped the phone from one ear to the other and tucked it into her shoulder. "Nothing's going on. He didn't say much. Roberto apparently called him. But by the time Leo arrived, it was already too late." Silence. "By the way, Leo saw his room...."

"Wow. That must've blown him away."

"And then some. Look, I don't want to talk about it right now. He may walk in and—"

"Sure, sure. You're right. My mind started racing when I saw him. Did he say anything about the house? Did you ask what he's planning on doing?"

Chicho gave her more random pieces. "It came up, and he seems unsure. He first said maybe sell, but what I saw in his eyes was internal conflict. Then he said something about not being in a rush. I guess he was trying to say that he's not going to just kick us out tomorrow."

"I think you need to ask him straight out so you know," Lola said.

"What am I gonna ask? Hey, can me and my son live in your home since I don't have a job and a place to live?"

"Yeah, something like that would be truthful."

"Well, I'm not gonna do that. We'll move."

"I don't wanna leave, Mama," Chicho said, still focused on his blocks.

Crap. She didn't want him to worry about this.

"Do you want me to speak to my principal and see if they still have that admin spot for you? There's only a few weeks left in summer, so it may be a stretch."

"No, I don't think so."

"Why not? Asking a question won't hurt. I even have an extra room in my apartment. You guys can stay with me until you sort things out."

Cat took a deep breath. "I need something local. I can't move away. Not yet, anyway."

"But it's still in the same state. I thought—"

"Nope. The leash is tight on me. The court restricted me to Fortuny Bay and only Fortuny Bay."

Silence. "Well, crap," Lola breathed.

"My feelings, exactly."

Chapter Thirteen

Leo

Leo pulled out the laptop from his luggage, connected it to the truck's Wi-Fi, and scanned through emails. He wasn't really interested in what was in his inbox. If there was anything important, Anna would call him. What he needed was a distraction. Anything to take his mind off of what he'd just seen and heard.

He leaned his head back and breathed in. There it was again. Her scent in his car. He'd often imagined what she looked like now. He didn't need to wonder anymore. She was more attractive than ever. He rolled down the windows. He needed to clear his mind.

His father had not once shown care or concern. Was he just limited by his inability to show emotion? Had he, in fact, actually cared for Leo all along?

He chuckled at the absurdity of it all. Even his own name was his way of creating a distance from his father. He had legally changed his name from Lionel junior to Leo. That's how petty he'd become.

How stupid and childish.

His instant messenger pinged. It was Anna.

Anna: Why are you online?

Leo: Catching up.

Anna: Call?

Crap. She wanted to talk.

Leo: Sure.

As soon as he hit enter, his phone rang.

"Hey, Anna."

"How are you holding up?"

A pause. "Okay, for the most part." He tapped the steering wheel.

"Did you go to the convalescent clinic?"

"Yeah, I did. He wanted to be cremated."

"Do you want me to help?" Anna asked, always ready to jump in.

"No. You won't believe this, but... do you remember when I told you about my ex, Cat?"

"Yes, of course, I remember Cat. I recall all the details that you dumped all over me when we first started working together."

"I did not dump anything," he said.

"Five hours, Leo. Five."

"A slight exaggeration. But anyway, let me get to the point. She's here."

"What do you mean by here? In Fortuny Bay?"

"In my parents' home. She's been taking care of my father. She. Lives. Here! And get this—she has a kid. A five-year-old boy."

"No way. So she's married?" she asked.

"Was. She's a widow."

"Oh man, that sucks," Anna said.

He hesitated. Now that he thought about it, it did suck. Presumably, she'd been in love with her husband. Why marry otherwise? She was left alone, and that poor kid would never know his dad. Then again, if his dad was anything like Leo's...

"So, is she taking care of the arrangements?" Anna asked, pulling Leo back into the conversation.

"Yeah, she's on it."

Silence. "Wow. How was it? To see her for the first time since leaving. Did you get all weak-kneed?" She laughed.

"I don't get weak-kneed." He hesitated. "It was weird, to be honest. At first, it was like—holy crap, it's Cat! Then when she was all pissed at me, it was like—holy crap, it's Cat! Ya'know what I mean?"

"Yeah, I feel you."

"I love it when you speak your age and not the old soul you were born into."

"Thanks," she said. "Why was she upset, exactly? Was it because you didn't get there in time?"

Leo pressed a button, and the bucket seat leaned him back. "No, not exactly. She was pissed that I left my father's life and had not checked in. Apparently, he'd been sick for three years."

"Ouch. I see. But she knows the history, yeah?"

"Yes, and no. Time has this amazing ability to take out a laser-tipped eraser and wipe out memory cells." He hesitated. "Make a note of that. I want to explore if there's science to back up the ability to erase memories. That's a trillion-dollar idea."

"Can you please focus?"

"Right. Anyway, from her perspective, she saw and knew the man that she'd been taking care of for the last three years. So she has a different perspective now."

"So... a changed man? Maybe realized he'd been wrong?"

He closed his eyes. "Are you sitting down?"

"Does it matter?"

"No, not really. Cat showed me my old room. It was left exactly the way I'd left it ten years ago. I mean, everything was as is. But it was meticulously cleaned. So, not abandoned, but maintained."

"What the actual—?"

"My sentiment exactly."

Silence joined them.

"What does this mean? Did you totally misread him?"

"No. No way. He was a mean old man; even when he wasn't trying to be mean, he was mean. But maybe the guy didn't know how to be any other way. I don't know."

More silence.

"So, Cat was mad at you because you were an absent son?"

"I suppose. But between us, as she told me what he was going through over those years, it became very clear that if he had money, he could've possibly had better medical treatment. Maybe, just maybe, with a better medical team, they could've cracked the code and had him healed."

"Ouch."

He caught movement from outside the house. It was Cat and Chicho. She was messing with the rusted, spiderweb-covered barbecue.

"I better go. She's outside." A pause. "What is she doing with that barbecue?"

"People typically use those devices to cook food. Not everyone has barbecues installed for their aesthetic look."

"Funny. You should be a comedian. After you've been laid off."

She laughed. "Promises, promises. How's the house? And what are you going to do with it?"

"House is okay. Old. In need of major work. But I'll probably sell it. If I can detach myself from the memories and the family history in it. First thing will be to get my hands on the deeds, etc."

"I'll help with that," she said. "While I wait for your next billion-dollar idea, I can track it. Shoot me the address."

He typed away. "Done."

"I'll let you know what I find out. Are you planning to stay in town?"

"Yeah."

"Do you need a hotel?"

He hesitated. "Well, my room is my room."

"Your ex lives there."

"In my house," Leo countered in a weak attempt at righteousness. "Yeah, you're right," he said. "Let me know what's available around here. And I'll see how it goes with Cat."

"You could always sleep in the Cybertruck. I bet camp mode in that car is amazing."

His eyes lit up. "That actually sounds awesome."

She laughed. "Later, Leo."

He hopped out of the car and strolled up to Cat. Chicho intercepted him.

"I love hot dogs," he said.

"Who doesn't?" Leo said.

Cat turned to him. "Are you hungry?" she asked. The setting sun illuminated her, causing her to practically glow.

His stomach grumbled. Those stupid seagulls had stolen his lunch, and the French fries hadn't done the job. He nodded.

"Dogs will have to do for now. The fridge is sort of empty. Did not have a chance to go to the grocery store these past few days."

"I'll go to the market," Leo said.

"Me too! Me too," Chicho said.

Leo looked at the little man, then turned to Cat. "If mom says okay, we can all go after we eat."

Francisco turned to his mom, his expression hopeful.

"Yeah, that's fine."

Chicho yelped.

Chapter Fourteen

Leo

Leo and Chicho went inside to grab plates and drinks while Cat grilled the hot dogs. Everything was exactly where he remembered them. He stared at the plastic plates with the faded flower patterns that, at some point in their life, were vibrant and colorful, but now, they barely held onto the image that had been rendered on the plates decades ago. He grabbed three cups.

"I use this one," Chicho said, showing off his Spider-Man cup.

"Good to know," he said, and returned one of the cups to the cupboard.

They walked through the laundry area to go back to the side of the house when an article of clothing caught his eye. In the basket of clean clothes was his red Stanford sweater. He wore that for the majority of his senior year of high school. But when he left, he left the sweater in the hamper of dirty clothes. Stanford had said no to him. No point in advertising a school that rejected him.

He touched the sweater and studied it to make sure this was indeed one and the same. Most of the color and texture had faded, but it sure looked like his. Why was it in the laundry, he wondered.

"We shouldn't leave the door open because bugs can get in," Chicho said.

Leo snapped toward his voice. "Sorry. You're right." Leo sped toward the open door and exited the house with Chicho.

Cat placed the dogs on the table as they arrived. Boy, his nutritionist would have a heart attack if she knew what he was about to eat. But when in Rome....

As they all sat, Cat took Chicho's hand, and Chicho took Leo's hand. For a moment, he didn't understand what was happening. Then he saw them lower their heads.

"Father, thank you for this meal. Thank you for your provisions. We pray for Lionel senior. May he rest in peace. In Jesus' name we pray. Amen."

"Amen," Chicho said, then glanced at Leo.

Leo hesitated, then mumbled something that sounded like Amen. *When did she start praying*, he wondered.

They each grabbed a bun and a dog.

"So, you like Spider-Man?" Leo asked Chicho.

"Yes. He's the best."

"I like Spider-Man too. I also like Batman. Do you like him?"

Cat interrupted. "Don't speak when you're eating. You don't want to choke on the food, right?"

"Right," Chicho said.

Leo hadn't even thought about that. "Sorry."

Just as he took a bite of the oh-so-unhealthy-but-oh-so-wonderful hotdog, Chicho tapped his arm.

"Mom says Batman just uses his money. He's not a real superhero."

Leo stared at her. "Is that right?"

She did not make eye contact, but he could see the smirk.

"He also uses his money to help people," Leo said. "He builds hospitals and schools. So in a way, he's a real hero."

Silence.

"Momma, are the Rocas super heroes?"

Cat stopped eating. Looked at her son. "No, they are not. Finish your meal so that we can go to the supermarket."

"Okay," he said and ate again.

He'd seen that name in the city. He didn't want to agitate her by asking questions, so instead, he focused on the dog.

He sipped the ice tea and scanned around. The air was super nice. Yeah, it was a bit hot, but that's how summer went around here. The beautiful sound of the ocean waves, the melodious combination of wind and wave and birds, took him back to when he and his mom would hike the five-minute path to the beach and hang out all day. He played in the water while she read or drew.

What happened to her art? Even as a kid, he knew her art was good. Real good. She painted in acrylic and water. If she had access to technology, she would've taken on that medium as well. He wondered if her drawings were stored somewhere. There was no way his father would've parted with those.

"Chicho, help mom clean up," Cat said, snapping Leo out of his memories.

"Then we take the spaceship to the store?"

"Yes, sir," Leo said.

Chicho laughed. "I'm not a sir," he said and continued chuckling.

"No? Then what are you?" Leo asked, playing his part.

"I'm a kid," he replied, as if he was speaking to someone who had missed out on the fundamentals of life.

Leo smiled, and when he looked up at Cat, he caught her smiling too.

"C'mon, little man," she said, and off they went.

He couldn't recall the last time he'd eaten this type of meal. Maybe his first year in college before he got noticed. There was something romantic about those days of cheese pizza, Mountain Dew, and video games. He missed those days.

⌇

Once out on the porch, Cat stepped up to him. "Maybe we shouldn't take your car. He needs a booster seat. Let's go with your dad's truck. I got one in there already."

"But Mom, I want to go with that one."

Leo looked at her, confused. "Get the booster seat and put it in mine."

She broke eye contact. "It may scuff up your leather seats."

He waited for the punchline. "And?"

She tipped her head. "You okay with that?"

"Well, yeah. It's just a car. Things will eventually get old in it. Let's go."

She studied his eyes for a moment, then strolled to the old truck while Leo and Chicho sauntered over to the Cybertruck.

"Wow," Chicho said when he reached the truck. "This is amazing," he said. He studied the oversized monitor and all the lights that welcomed him in.

"It is a cool toy," Leo admitted.

Chicho laughed again. "This is not a toy."

Man, kids take things so literally.

Cat brought the seat, and Leo installed it in the middle spot. Chicho would sit between them.

"Ready?"

"Ready," Chicho said.

To add to the drama, Leo gave the car a voice command, and the monitor showed where they were going. Finally, he allowed the self-driving mode to take them there.

"It's driving on its own?" Chicho asked, his mouth agape.

"It sure is." He turned to Cat, but she was not smiling.

The grocery store had been updated a bit. The name was now "Roca," like so many other things in the city. He needed to ask Cat about that.

They got a bunch of stuff from each aisle, including the best beer this place offered. He and Chicho were about to add some more items when Cat stopped them.

"That's enough things, guys," she said.

Leo studied her. "What's the matter?" he asked. He assumed she knew he was paying.

She clenched her jaw. "You forget the size of the refrigerator at the house. All this won't fit."

He blinked. "Then I guess we'll have to get a new fridge, too. Who sells refrigerators here?"

"It's not that simple, Leo," she said, her face flushed.

"Sure it is. We go, we pick, we buy, they deliver."

"Is it that easy, Mama?" Chicho asked.

"Only for some people," she said, her voice icy, her face stoic. "Fine. Drop us off, and you go do what you want to do."

They finished up, paid for the groceries, and went back to the truck. He didn't get her. What was the issue? He wanted to say a few choice words, but kept his mouth shut until they got back to the house.

Once back home and Chicho was out of earshot, he tapped her shoulder. "Is there a problem?"

She put down the box of eggs on the counter and faced him. "You really want to know?"

"Well, yeah. That's why I asked."

"Fine." She took a step closer to him and lowered her voice. "I don't want Chicho to be confused. He is being bombarded with things. A lot of things. Expensive cars. Futuristic cars. Unlimited groceries. New appliances on demand. Buy what you want, when you want. It's not right."

"It's not right?" He grinned, but it wasn't a friendly one. He was getting a bit upset. "It's actually *very* right. I worked my ass off to get to where I am. I built companies and technologies that I am proud of. I have money. Lots of it. I won't apologize for my success either. When I spend it, it helps the businesses I'm buying from. They take my money, and they're able to keep little Johnny employed. There is nothing wrong with what I'm doing."

She shook her head. "You missed the point. As usual. What happens when we leave this house? What happens when he's back to being poor? Let's be honest; with me, he will be poor. Maybe—eventually—we can get to a point in our lives where we have a middle-class lifestyle. But we will *never* have your lifestyle. It's unfair to the kid. He will come to hope and expect. But when I can't provide that? Then what?"

He didn't know what to say to that. She was right. And it broke his heart that she said they would be poor.

"Look," he said, his voice low. "I can help you to—"

"I don't need anything. I have everything I need." Her voice had taken an edge.

"Okay, I'm not trying to insult you."

"Then don't offer again. I can figure it out."

He hesitated. "What I'm saying is that you have a place to stay. Right here. I'm not rushing anything. So you don't have to assume it's imminent. I don't want you guys to be in a state of despair."

She breathed in, then nodded. "Thank you. A slower transition will help Chicho... and me."

An uncomfortable silence inserted itself into the kitchen.

"Do you have luggage?" she asked, shifting the topic. "As you saw, your room is ready. It's been waiting for your return."

He thought about it for a nanosecond. "It may be best if I give you some room. This is a bit too much, too quick. For both of us."

"This is your house—" she started.

"I know. But I think for today, it would be best if I stay at a hotel."

She smiled. "There are no hotels here."

"None?"

"The city council has not approved any hotels. They don't approve much."

"Airbnb?"

She laughed. "The city council made it illegal a few years back."

He scratched his head. "I see."

A beat.

"Look, you do what you feel comfortable doing. Your room is yours," she said, then continued to load the rusty turd of an excuse for a fridge. The light bulb flickered.

"Okay, your fair point of mixed messaging notwithstanding, this fridge is horrible. I need to replace it."

"It's your home," she mumbled.

"Where can I go get one?"

"Roca's TV & Appliances," she said.

"There's that name again. Who is this Roca?"

She glanced at him. "You don't remember them? That family's been here forever. As long as your family, probably. But they didn't start branding their businesses until shortly after you left. The Roca family owns practically all of Fortuny Bay. When they sneeze, the people ask them for forgiveness."

His eyes went wide. "Tell me that's a joke."

She shook her head. "No joke. As far as you're concerned, they are Fortuny Bay."

Chapter Fifteen

Leo

Once outside, Leo took a deep breath of the coastal air. The scents of the beach were downright invigorating, unlike the harbor, which smelled like fish guts. He always loved the beach, but it wasn't until he moved away and visited other beaches like Malibu and Pismo that he realized this beach town was not really a beach town at all. The beach's existence was acknowledged, but it wasn't part of the culture and lifestyle. Unlike places like Pismo, where all were centered on beach life. It wasn't an afterthought—it was the theme of the town.

His phone rang. It was Anna.

"Hey, what's up?" he asked.

"The closest hotel is thirty minutes away."

He scoffed. "Yeah, I heard. Odd, isn't it, that they'd have nothing here?"

"For sure, particularly when you consider how hot it is up and down PCH to live in and visit towns that are within walking distance to the water."

He couldn't remember anyone talking about Fortuny being a touristy area. He stopped himself. No, that wasn't true. His father used to say that this place could never be as beautiful as the French Riviera, but could easily compete with the Santa Barbaras of the world.

Then why not? Why stick to commercial fishing only?

"So, Chris and I did a bit of digging on your dad's—your—property. This may be wrong, so we've asked for records from the county assessor."

"What are you talking about? I missed something."

"Online records are great for newer homes or at least active homes. This house has not been bought or sold since the late 1800s, so the records on the internet are sparse at best. But if what we suspect is right, the property is not just the house. The property extends all the way to the beach. You are potentially sitting on a good twenty acres of prime real estate."

"Wait, what? Twenty acres?"

"Sure seems like it. If you're good with it, I can reach out to Sophie, your property attorney, to pull records for you."

He scanned the horizon all the way to the beach. Did he really own all of this? Is that why his father wanted to open a B&B? Did he see this potential as a tourist magnet?

Forget bed-and-breakfast. That was small-town thinking. Leo saw it as both a tourist magnet but also, since the land was so large, over time, it could become a resort. He immediately saw the financial potential. Someone he met at an event recently bought a resort in San Diego for 400 million dollars. There was real money in resorts. Prime real estate had the potential to exponentially multiply wealth while reducing the taxable footprint. This was very interesting, indeed.

"Good work, Anna. Let me know what details Sophie pulls. Also, reach out to the architect she introduced us to at the tennis tournament in New York."

"You mean Pete?" she asked. "Pete Nicos?"

"That's him."

"I'm on it. What are you going to do tonight? Will you stay at your house?"

He glanced back at the dilapidated structure. "Nah, I'm going to camp in my truck."

"I bet it'll be awesome."

"I'll let you know tomorrow."

Chapter Sixteen

Catalina

Through the threaded kitchen curtain, Cat watched Leo on his phone. Always busy, reeling and whealing and whatever it was that he did. He marched with such confidence and self-assuredness. He always had that swagger. She did, too, a long time ago. But over time, she lost most of her footing. Until Lionel senior took her in. It took time—years—but she found her center again. Her North Star.

She washed the last dish, placed it on the dish rack, and dried her hands with the rag. She took one more quick peek at Leo. He was now jumping into his ridiculous car. What was he compensating for by driving that thing?

She wanted to laugh at her own wit, but she knew better. The only thing that guy lacked was family. Everything else he was covered. She envied him on some level. Not his money and the things he had. But the freedom by which he lived.

She had no such luxury.

She locked the doors, checked all the windows, turned off the lights, then checked the gas range. Before she went upstairs, she checked the doors and windows one more time.

When would this habit die? When would she have peace—real peace—again? When would her husband's family leave her alone? When would the court see through all this and say enough? How would she earn money to pay for basic necessities?

She did not have answers. But she had a lot of questions. And she made sure she asked all of her questions during her daily prayer walks around the house. She believed God was listening to her. He just wasn't giving her straightforward answers. But on some level, she felt He was not answering her because He was protecting her.

That gave Cat comfort. That was the only thing that comforted her.

She walked upstairs and entered their room to check on Chicho. He was fast asleep. That did not surprise her. He'd been awake all day with no naps in between. She gently took off his clothes and slipped on his PJs. When he went out, he was out completely. Nothing could wake him.

Once changed, she tucked him under the sheets and planted a kiss on his forehead. "God bless you," she whispered.

He was a good boy. A blessing, no doubt. A little angel placed in her life to give her balance, hope, and joy. She was about to turn off the bedroom light when she saw a new drawing on his table. She loved his drawings. The kid had a gift. One day she'd get him real lessons and art supplies.

She picked it up and studied it. This drawing caught her off guard. He'd drawn Leo's truck. He had also drawn Leo standing in front of the nose of the truck and Cat holding Chicho's hand at the tail of the truck. Sitting in the truck's bed was what looked like a refrigerator.

It was happening already. Chicho was gravitating to the things that they did not have, but Leo did. This was not healthy for him. It would only end in sadness.

She set the drawing back on the table, then left the room. She did not close the door. He did not like being trapped.

She went downstairs, grabbed the finished laundry, and took it to the kitchen table. On top was her old sweater.

She hesitated. Had Leo seen it? Cat did not want him to ask questions about why she had an identical Stanford sweater like the one he had all those years ago.

She picked it up, recalling his. She brought it to her face and pressed her cheek onto it like she used to do before. When he lay on the grass, and she placed her head on his chest as they both dreamt of the future. She quickly buried it to the bottom of the basket, not wanting Leo to see it and ask questions. His dreams had materialized. Hers had turned into a persistent nightmare.

[illegible]
[illegible]
[illegible]
[illegible]
[illegible]

[illegible]
[illegible]
[illegible]
[illegible]

Chapter Seventeen

Leo

Leo visited the local appliance store, but the place was, at best, pitiful. And the salesperson was, at best, confused.

"How about this one?" Leo asked, pointing to a basic refrigerator.

"Oh, I need to check, but I think they can deliver it in like two weeks," the sales guy said.

"Two weeks," Leo said, more to himself.

"Yeah. Sorry, man. I think it's because of supply chain issues."

Leo nodded and pulled out his phone.

"The thing is that we don't really sell a lot of refrigerators, so we don't have them in stock," the guy added.

Leo tapped, typed, and continued nodding.

"But if you want to pay expedited fees, maybe I can improve on that by a couple of days."

"So here's the thing," Leo said. "I just ordered a fridge from a national chain, and they will deliver it tomorrow."

"Oh wow. Are you sure?"

Leo sighed, then showed him his order confirmation.

"Shoot, I guess you won't need to buy it from here now."

"Good guess," Leo said. "Thanks anyway." As he walked out, he saw an older man approach the salesperson.

Good. Maybe they'll learn how competition works.

He entered his car, frustrated. He'd hoped to roll the new fridge into his truck and take it home. But he would have to wait.

As he pulled into his property, he saw that most of the lights were out. He pulled the truck onto the side of the house and then decided to drive the path that he and his mom used to walk. If this land was really his, he could do whatever he pleased.

His truck easily maneuvered through the terrain. And even though it was late, his headlights lit up the path perfectly. He stopped halfway there. The full moon was lighting up the ocean beautifully. From this slightly elevated vantage point, he was just high enough to see an amazing perspective. This would be a perfect place to build a resort. The rooms with this view could pull major cash.

He decided this spot was as good as any to make camp. A couple of commands and the seats flattened into a full bed. He set the car in camping mode, and the car generated enough heat to keep him comfortable. He changed into comfy clothes and slid into the sleeping bag.

He stared up through the full-glass roof of the truck. The sky was spray-painted with stars.

He remembered that night. The first time with Cat. It was well past midnight, and a small fire kept them warm. They nestled into each other inside the worn sleeping bag. The cold evening was suddenly warm, and beautiful, and perfect. They kissed, they nibbled, and then they melted into each other. They made promises. At that time, he did not know that he would not be able to keep them.

He smiled. Those were good days. They were together, and they were happy. But life threw him a curveball, and he needed more from life than what this place could offer. He couldn't be limited to this town and to small aspirations. And now, having seen what had happened to this town over the last decade, it was clear that he'd done the right thing. There was no future here.

But had he done the right thing with her?

"You told me you loved me," she had said to him when he told her he was leaving.

The look in her eyes said what he hoped she would not assume— that he said what she wanted to hear just so he could be with her.

No matter what she thought, he had loved her. He had never loved anyone since.

That was the truth that now seemed meaningless. He'd broken her heart, and now she was where she was. A single parent, a widow, poor.

He rubbed his face, then turned sideways and closed his eyes. But he could not clear his mind of her face. She was as beautiful as ever. When they were younger, she lit up the room when she entered. She changed the atmosphere. She'd lost some of her fire, but that was just because of her current circumstance. She still had it. How odd that although he'd been with models and celebrities, his past flame still outshone all of them.

He wondered what she was doing now? Was she asleep? Or was she also awake thinking of the past?

Chapter Eighteen

Catalina

As was customary for her, she was awake at six in the morning. Since she'd moved into Lionel senior's home, she woke hours before he did to get her personal work done, exercise, clean, organize, and prepare for the day ahead. Back then, she had to plan for an ailing adult and a live wire toddler. Now she only had Francisco to think of. And the court hearings. And now Leo, of course.

She opened the fridge and was grateful that they had food in there. Fruits and peanut butter and so much more. Lionel was on a fixed income. And no matter what he told her, she knew what he had and what he didn't. She always found the most frugal way to make the dollar stretch. But with Leo... well, he didn't seem to even look at the price tag.

She pulled the box of strawberries and washed five pieces to have for breakfast. She couldn't recall the last time she had this type of luxury. No, that wasn't true. It was forty-two months ago. Just before her husband died. A handful of months before Lionel gave her a place to stay. She scanned the kitchen and wondered how long she could stay now that Lionel was gone.

Leo promised he would not be kicking them out anytime soon. That did not mean she could stay here, rent-free, for as long as she liked. Then again, what were the chances that he'd stay in Fortuny Bay? If she had to bet, she would guess that he would stay maybe until after the service, and then he'd leave and he'd forget about this place for months. If not years.

A ray of hope entered her heart. Maybe she'd be fine. Just enough time to get the court to see things her way, get herself back on her feet, and boom. She could then leave town, work at a place where she could grow. This was starting to sound hopeful.

She didn't hear the engine, but she heard crunching gravel. She peeked out of the window and saw the monster of a truck humming through the dirt path back into the driveway. Well... it wasn't really a driveway, was it? It was a sea of dirt all around the house. It had been years since cement or grass had been seen.

He opened the truck's door and leapt out. He was in his shorts and undershirt. His clothing disguised his physique. He looked ripped. She took a step backward to make sure he couldn't see her. What was she doing? Why was she spying on him? She walked back to the fridge and pulled out eggs and scrambled them.

The rusty screen door whined, and the kitchen door opened.

"Knock, knock," he whispered.

"G'mornin'," she said, in as nonchalant a way as possible.

"You're up early."

She glanced over her shoulder and swirled the butter in the hot pan. "Yeah, always up early. How did you sleep?"

"Pretty good, I guess."

She poured the eggs into the sizzling pan.

"You could've slept here," she said and faced him. "Eggs?"

"Yeah, sure. Thanks." He walked up to her. "The truck was super comfortable. That wasn't the issue."

"Oh?"

"Just kept waking up thinking about this place, the town... old memories."

She chuckled. "Yeah, well. When you stay away for that long, it's like stepping into a time loop."

He stepped right behind her, watching her finish off the eggs. His physical proximity to her made her feel a bit uncomfortable. She knew that feeling. She didn't want it.

"Smells different," he said.

She turned off the fire, then grabbed the pan's handle. "Your eggs smell different from these eggs?"

He grinned and gave her room as she split the eggs between two plates.

"Something smells different."

"Butter," she said.

He scoffed. "That's so bad for you."

"Not trying to make the cover of *Cosmo*. If you remain active, real butter is a great source of vitamin D."

"Have you heard of supplements?"

She stared at him. "Just shut up and have real food for once."

They both sat. He hesitantly forked a bit and placed it in his mouth like it would explode any second.

She added some salt and pepper and forked a big chunk into her mouth.

He was staring at her. When she swallowed, he swallowed. Then something happened in his eyes. He forked a bit more and chewed. Then more and more.

"That's right. Real eggs with real butter. You'll do well to stay away from tofu burgers and soy coffee."

He finished it up without saying a word. His eyes glimmered.

She hesitated. "What's wrong, Leo?"

He shook his head. "Nothing's wrong. It's just... totally reminded me of mom. That's how her eggs tasted." He breathed deep. "That was a real treat. Thanks, Cat."

She grinned. "You're welcome. By the way, the shower across your old room has fresh towels if you want to use it."

He rose and took his plate to the sink. "Don't want to wake up the little dude. I'm gonna get some work done—for the company—then come back in a couple of hours. Will that work?"

She nodded.

He was about to leave when he hesitated at the door. "Did you have some other job, too?"

"No. My job was to care for your dad."

He considered that.

"Okay, well... if I can help—"

"I'm going to look and see how that goes."

He turned to face her. "Locally?"

She shrugged her shoulders. "Ideally, but we'll see."

"Not too many jobs here?"

She crossed her arms. "There are always jobs here. But somehow, I have never been qualified enough."

"What does that mean?"

She tucked a strand of loose hair behind her ear. "I have apparently rubbed some people the wrong way. So it's always a bit more challenging."

He grinned. "You? Rub people the wrong way? With that sunny disposition of yours. Hard to believe."

She did her best to hide her smile. "I thought you had to leave."

"Yeah. See you later," he said.

"Later."

He opened the door, sauntered out, and the screen door shut behind him.

She washed her dish, and when she put it away, she glanced around the kitchen. Something was wrong. But she couldn't put her finger on it. No, it wasn't Lionel senior's absence.

She paused. Suddenly, she was overcome with a familiar emotion. One she hadn't felt for over a decade.

She missed Leo.

Chapter Nineteen

Leo

Leo hopped in his truck and drove into town. Technically, he could've done the work he needed to do from the house. But he needed to create a bit of space between them, both literally and metaphorically. He was feeling things. Not sure he wanted to classify said feelings, but he knew that distance was a wise choice.

Leo glanced at the charge level of his car's battery. He'd have to get the truck charged soon. He hadn't seen electrical car charging stations, but it didn't hurt to ask around. The first gas station was a bust. And the second gas station didn't fare any better. The high schooler fixing another car's blown tire was too busy staring at the truck instead of listening to Leo's question.

When he pulled out of the station, twirling red and blue lights from behind him stopped his progress. He looked into the rearview mirror and saw the sheriff's squad car behind him.

"Well, crap," he said as he pulled over. Had he done anything that was illegal? He didn't think so.

He rolled the window down and waited.

"Take your sweet time, why don't you?" he whispered to himself.

Leo studied the reflection of the man behind him through the truck's side mirror. The deputy stepped out, adjusted his sunglasses, his hat, and then his holster. He strolled slowly and then finally came face to face with Leo.

"What seems to be the problem, Deputy?" Leo asked.

The man stared at him for a few seconds. "You mean other than the fact that you're a jerk?" the deputy responded.

Leo's eyes went wide. "I'm sorry... what was that?"

The man removed his glasses.

A beat.

They both broke into laughter.

"Billy? Did they seriously give you a gun?" Leo said, then opened the door and hopped out.

They embraced, slapping each other's backs.

"I heard you were in town," Billy said, "so I figured I might as well mess with you."

"Well done. So you're the law now? Do they know about your past?" Leo asked, gesturing air quotes when he said past.

Billy pointed at him. "Unless you want to spend some time in a ten-by-ten cell, you'll want to keep them lies to yourself."

"They'll go to the grave with me." A moment passed between them.

"Sorry about your pa. I know you two weren't close and all, even so, you know... he's family."

Leo broke eye contact and glanced at his surroundings. "Yeah, appreciate it." An uncomfortable silence joined them.

"Where were you headed to?" Billy asked.

"Well, was hoping to find an electrical charging station."

Billy nodded to the truck. "For this beast?"

"Yup."

"Some folk have it in their homes. But no public ones. The City Council rejected the motion."

Leo shook his head. "Okay, I'm not even gonna try to understand that. I was going to find a place to drink coffee. Do you have time to grab a cup?"

"Not free this morning, unfortunately, but follow me, and I'll take you to the spot with the best cup of coffee in town."

They arrived at a breakfast and lunch place that Leo did not recognize. They walked in together.

"Mornin' Billy," the server called. "For two?" She had a gentle smile about her, but also a hint of something else in the way she smiled at Billy.

He reciprocated the smile. "No, Barb, just for my long-lost friend Lionel, here." He placed his hand on Leo's shoulder. "Get him the fresh stuff. He's a big city kid."

They shook hands one more time, and then Billy left. But as he passed the glass window, he waved at Barb one more time.

Leo liked what he saw between them.

"Lionel, is it?" she asked as he sat.

"Leo, actually."

She handed him a menu.

"You sort of look familiar."

"I have one of those faces," he said.

"Probably. So you're originally from here?"

"Yes, left some ten years ago."

"So just visiting?"

"For a few days."

She smiled. "Well, I'm sure Billy and your other friends are thrilled to see you. So, what can I get you—other than coffee?"

He knew he shouldn't, but he'd seen them in the display case. "Are those croissants filled with anything?"

"The top row has chocolate in them. The two below are my personal favorites. Filled with Nutella. Have you tried those before?"

His mouth watered. Yes, he had become addicted to Nutella after college, and it continued to be his weakness.

"I'll take the two you have in the display case."

Her eyes lit up with joy. "I like you already. You got it."

Chapter Twenty

Leo

Leo was deep into his second pastry and third cup of coffee, brainstorming new business ideas on his tablet, when he heard the door open. Immediately, the staff began rustling and the surrounding conversations dropped to a hush.

"Good morning," a woman from behind the cash register said a little too loudly.

Leo turned his attention to the older woman that had walked in. Her silver hair was perfectly styled and cut short. Her outfit was not meant for this town. She could've been part of the socialite class in San Francisco or Manhattan. She wore a double-breasted black pantsuit. Pinned to her chest was a gold brooch with an emblem he recognized from his early days. She was declaring her pedigree—a Spaniard. One of the originals.

She was flanked by two extremely large men. Dark sunglasses, chests and shoulders that stretched the threads of their suits to their maximum tension. And if he was right, the bulge inside their coats was not their King James Bible. They were security, and they were packing.

Who the heck is she?

Just as he completed that thought, she turned and faced him. Her red lipstick was a stark contrasted against the white powdered cheeks. She stretched her lips into a half-smile. She ambled up to his table. He set his coffee down.

"You must be Lionel Moncrieff junior," she said, her voice multiple notches younger than her face. There was an iciness to it. A precision that he'd only seen in boardrooms.

He rose and extended a hand. "Leo," he said. She placed her perfectly manicured hand in his. A quick shake. "Would you like to join me?" he asked.

She sat, then smiled and said nothing more. Just studied his face.

"I am at a disadvantage. You know me, but I must admit I don't know you."

She smiled graciously. "I wouldn't expect you to. You were rather young when you were here." She chuckled. "You still are."

Leo studied her, waiting for her to offer her name.

Just then, Barb gingerly slid a gold-rimmed bone china teacup and saucer in front of the woman. She placed a matching teakettle next to her cup. "Mrs. Roca, shall I—" Barb started to say, but the woman lifted her hand in the gesture that said, 'no and leave' in one swift move. Barb disappeared.

Roca. The name that was plastered on every other building in Fortuny Bay.

They are *Fortuny Bay as far as you're concerned*, Cat had said.

Roca plucked the teakettle from the table and poured some tea into her cup. A fruity aroma lofted toward Leo.

"Mrs. Roca," he said. "I've seen your name all over town. It's nice to meet you," he said.

"Adela. Please call me Adela."

He took a sip of his coffee just as she sipped her tea. He waited her out. She wanted something from him. It was her move.

"First, let me express my condolences," she finally said. "Although I didn't know your father well, he was part of the long history of this town that I call home. He was a fixture." Another sip. "He will be missed."

He didn't believe her. "I appreciate that."

"And your mom," she started. "She and the Casa family were practically royalty here. We miss Cèlia."

That, he believed. "That's very kind."

"Will you be staying in Fortuny Bay for long?"

He spun his mug. "No, not long. Just until everything is settled."

She didn't react, but he'd seen enough gamblers to know that this was the news she expected. Solid poker face.

"I know who you are, Lionel."

"Leo," he said again.

She grinned. "I know who you are, Leo. I know you are a busy man. Therefore, I am happy to have my people—from the bank, to the mortuary, to realtors, to whatever you may need—to assist you. They are at your disposal."

He found her choice of services to call out interesting.

"Thank you, Mrs. Roca, but—"

"Adela," she corrected.

It was his turn to grin. "Thank you, Adela. Thankfully, I have someone who can help with all those things."

"Miss Catalina Alonzo," she stated. A dryness in her tone.

"That's right."

She finished her tea in one long sip. The tea was still steaming, but she downed it like it was a beer contest.

She placed the cup down and rose. Leo got to his feet as well. "Good. I am happy to hear that." She took a step back, but hesitated. "You will want to keep close to the details."

Leo's brows scrunched. "What does that mean?"

She seemed to consider her words. "I know that Miss Alonzo was very close to your father. Almost like a daughter." Her right eyebrow twitched. Leo didn't know how to interpret what that tell meant. Her expression was well-guarded. "I am not one to understand or bother with those matters. People do what they need to do because life's circumstances lead them to those roads."

He ran a hand through his hair. "I'm not sure I understand."

"No, I suppose you don't. The good book tells us to not gossip. Therefore, I will repeat what I initially recommended. You will want to keep close to the details."

She turned and walked to the door. One of her bodyguards opened the door for her.

"Have a good day, Mrs. Roca," the owner of the cafe said, clearly nervous.

Adela turned to her. "You, too, dear." She glanced at Leo and smiled. "Hope to see you again," she said and strode out.

He watched her enter a brand new Bentley and speed away.

Leo dropped back into his seat. *What was that about?*

Barb showed up at the table and took Adela's kettle and cup. "I get so nervous when she comes," she said.

"Why?"

Barb held his gaze. "When the owner gets nervous, the rest of us get worried too. From what I understand, Roca is the one who gave the loan to open this place."

"You mean the Roca bank, right?"

She shrugged. "Is there a difference? It's still her." She excused herself and left him alone.

He didn't want to burn brain cells on Adela and the situation in this town. But his gut instinct was now activated. Something was not right.

What was Cat really up to?

You will want to keep close to the details, Adela had said, twice.

He grabbed his tablet and left the cafe. Unhealthy thoughts interrupted him during the short drive back to the house.

His father always liked Cat. He called her 'the one thing you did right.' Had she used that relationship to get a free ride out of him? It sure seemed that way, and based on what Adela, the Doña Roca, had said, she wanted him to know that there was more to the situation than met the eye. She practically implied that he should not trust Cat.

He took a left and sped up the hill toward his family home. Had Cat taken advantage of a lonely, sick old man who needed help?

As he pulled into the dirt driveway, he shook his head. That's not who she'd been in the past. She'd always been a decent person. Too good for him, in fact. But sometimes, desperate times caused the best of them to sink to lower levels.

As he rolled out of his truck, he remembered his sweater. Why had she cleaned it? Why had she put it right in front of him? Was she trying to start something to assure her place in this home?

He recalled the conversation earlier. Was she manipulating him to let her stay?

He didn't like being played with. He ran up the steps and marched into the kitchen.

Chapter Twenty-One

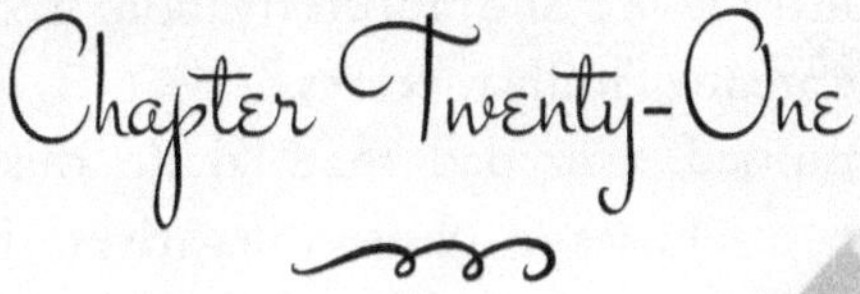

Catalina

Two hours in, and Cat had barely made a dent in the containers of pictures. Boxes with old photographs, envelopes that housed the negatives, piles of picture frames, and reels of slides. Thankfully, Lola had taken Francisco with her to the park to play basketball, which gave Cat space and time to focus.

She heard the door open, and Leo yell, "Cat!" The screen door slammed shut.

Now what?

She rose off the floor and stepped out of the study. "I'm here," she said, in as calm of a voice as possible.

They came face to face. He seemed to appraise her. Cat must've looked like she'd been wrestling with a monster-sized dust bunny. His eyes lingered momentarily on her bare thighs. He pulled his eyes back up to hers. "We need to talk," he said, his voice calmer.

"In there," she said and went back inside the study.

She dropped on the floor and continued with separating the material by approximate year.

He walked in and stopped at the entrance. "What are you doing?"

She blew a strand of hair out of her face. "Honestly, what I'm doing is digging myself into a hole." She tapped the floor next to her.

He sat. "These are my family pictures."

"Yeah. I'd promised your dad that I'd do this project for him months ago. There are boxes of photos, negatives, slides, you name it from generations." She searched through a pile and pulled one out. "Check this one out."

He studied the yellowed envelope, then slid out the photos. His eyes went wide. "How old are these?"

"My best guess, early 1900s when *Casa* was first built. These are your mom's grandparents, I think."

He brought the photos close to his face. "Are you kidding me?"

"Just look at me." He did. She knew she had smudges all over her face. "Do I look like I did all this just to kid you?"

He grinned. "No, guess not." He frowned. He handed her the envelope.

She reached behind her and grabbed another pile. She flipped through it, then pulled one and handed it to him.

Leo's eyes froze on the image. He couldn't have been more than seven or eight years old. He was sitting on his father's shoulders. His father held a firm grasp of his legs and wore something on his face that Leo did not recognize: a genuine smile. Next to them was his mom. Smiling ear to ear with Disneyland in the background. She was well back then. No illness. No sadness. A happy family.

Why couldn't he remember those times? Why did he only remember the sad days, the angry days.

"Looks like you guys had some good days as a family," Cat said, snapping Leo out of his thoughts.

"I suppose so," he said. He handed her the photo, then scanned the piles of content and thought of all the work that she'd have to do. "Why? I mean, I get you promised him something before he passed. But why now? You don't owe him this."

She flinched. "For one, my word matters. Also, I happen to believe that he's in heaven, watching over us."

He scoffed.

"Please, don't make fun of my beliefs."

He straightened. "Sorry. Didn't mean to demean you. It's just that...."

"I know. A combination of you don't think your dad would make it to heaven, you don't believe in heaven, or both."

He shrugged.

"Well, I do," she said. "And a promise is a promise."

He stared at her.

"So, I believe he's watching me, hoping I won't forget the promises I made him. Also, I figured you'd appreciate this. I know that when you left, you didn't take any of the past with you. Just a couple of pictures of you and your mom."

He leaned back against the couch in the study. "And how do you know that?"

She stopped looking at him. "It doesn't take a detective to see what pictures disappeared from your room when you left. I remember what used to be there and what you left behind."

He hesitated. "I took our prom picture, too."

She clenched her jaw. "Don't. Just don't do that."

"What?"

"I don't need a consolation prize. You left. You lied to me. You never came back."

He remained frozen. "You're right," he whispered.

A hesitation. "I know. I usually am," she said and offered a faint smile. He returned it.

"Anyhoo. I figured if I can organize these by general timeline, you would want to take it somewhere safe back wherever you live."

He snapped his fingers. "I have an idea that may help." He pulled out his phone and said, "Call Anna."

His phone dialed a number as he switched the phone to speaker mode.

"What's up, Jefe?" the woman on the other line said. Who was she, wondered Cat?

"Anna, I have you on speaker with Cat."

A pause. "Hi Cat, nice to speak with you."

"Same here."

"Here's the deal," Leo said. "Cat has boxes of old photos, negs, and more. I want a crew to come here to collect it, scan it at the highest resolution possible, store the originals in archival quality containers, then ship them out to where I have my other collectibles in Nevada."

"Sure thing," Anna said. "I'll get you an ETA by close of business."

"You're a lifesaver."

"Anything else?" she asked.

"Yeah, I need a charging station installed here. My truck's going to need juice eventually."

A hesitation. "How long are you planning on staying there?"

He scanned the ceiling for answers. "Well, I will return to San Jose soon, but I do plan to come back now and then. So, just like my other places, I want a supercharger available."

"So..." Anna started, but didn't finish.

"Spit it out."

"Not planning to sell?"

He looked into Cat's eyes. "No immediate plans."

"Clear. Well, Cat, it was nice chatting, but with Leo, it is almost impossible for anyone to get a word in—"

"Poor connection. Bye," Leo said.

"Ciao," Anna said, and they both cut the line.

She marveled at their conversation. She and Leo used to speak that way. A comfortable dance, back and forth. Were these two together, she wondered?

"Who is Anna?"

He rose. "My right-hand person. I have two right-hand people, but it's weird to call another person my left-hand person."

"It is weird." She also rose. "It looks like you just fired me from this project."

"No, not at all. The people who come will need context. You are probably the only one who is the closest to it. Other than me, that is."

"I have more context than you," she corrected.

"This is my family. I think I know better."

She was not convinced. "We'll just agree to disagree. What was your point about context?"

"Since you don't have a job, if you want to help with this, I'll pay you consulting fees to get these done right."

She wasn't sure how to read what he was offering. Was he taking pity on her? "I'm not a charity case."

"No. You're helping me document my heritage. That's important to me."

"Why? You never seemed to care before."

He hesitated. "I have no family that I know of. What if there are cousins that are somewhere in France or Spain? These may be the clue I would need."

She nodded. "Okay, fine."

"We haven't discussed terms," he said.

"I'll just have to trust that you pay better than minimum wage."

He put out his hand. "I do. Deal?"

"Deal," she said. She put her hand in his, and he shook it. At that moment, a familiar current transferred from his hand to hers. Her breath caught, and she thought she saw something in his eyes, too. But neither flinched nor pulled back. They remained connected for a few more seconds.

"Where's everyone?" Lola yelled from the kitchen.

"In here," Cat tried to say, but her voice caught.

He said, "In the study."

They released their hands just as she and Chicho walked in.

"What are you doing?" Chicho asked.

"Reliving history," Leo said.

He was right about that.

[illegible]
[illegible]
[illegible]
[illegible]
[illegible]
[illegible]
[illegible]
[illegible]

[illegible]
[illegible]
[illegible]
[illegible]
[illegible]

Chapter Twenty-Two

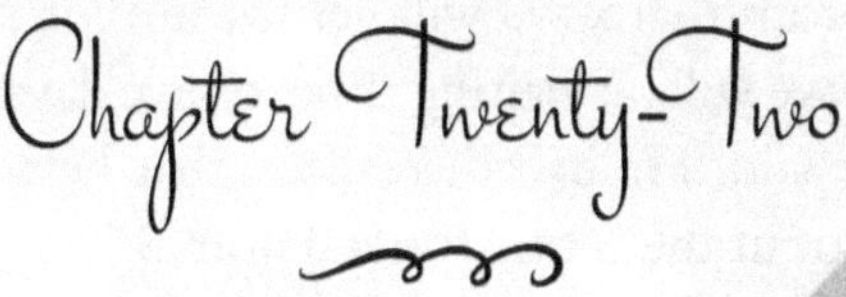

Leo

Leo pulled himself together. He couldn't get derailed by her proximity and her apparent care for his father. Yes, he appreciated this. She'd taken her promise seriously to organize and maintain the family photos. Even so, why would someone like Adela, who was clearly respected by the community, say what she had said? Was there more to this? There were still a lot of questions that he needed to ask, but what he did know was that Cat had cared for his father. That counted for a lot. He didn't see anything that gave Adela's words any weight.

Cat's phone rang. "Hi, Roberto," she said as she answered the phone.

Leo wondered what the attorney wanted.

"Yes, he's here," she said, eying Leo. "I'll pass it to him now."

She handed him her phone. When he put it to his ear, he picked up her scent. A natural perfume that had always been all Cat.

Aw man. This is getting too familiar.

He gathered himself. "Mr. Chaparral," Leo said as he left the study and moved into the kitchen. "Everything okay?"

"Yes, I wanted to give you a quick update on where we are with your father's remains. We have to wait for the death to be registered with the county. After that, the medical examiner will sign off on his death certificate. From there, we will get the authorization to cremate. So, at a minimum, we will be waiting three to five days."

"Oh wow," he said. He hadn't realized that he'd have to stay here that long. "What about the actual funeral home?"

"All arranged. Your father already had a spot next to your mother. So, they're just waiting for the paperwork, and then it'll be done."

He sat down on the kitchen chair. "Thank you for the update. If you need anything, Annabelle has complete authority to help you." Leo was not about to give the lawyer his direct number. You always needed a firewall. Most people took advantage of a direct relationship. Anna knew who to let through.

"That'll be great. I'll be in touch soon on some other matters, but I want to make sure this goes smoothly."

"Sounds like a plan," Leo said.

He hung up, then glanced at Cat's key chain on the kitchen table. Something caught his eye. He reached for it and saw his gold ring. The one that he'd given to her. It had lost most of its luster and was scratched up.

She's kept it. After all these years, she still has it.

Why, he wondered.

Did she...?

No. He would not go there. He arranged the keys the way they were and went back to the study.

He rejoined Cat, Lola, and Chicho and handed Cat the phone. He tried to make eye contact to see if there was anything there. But there wasn't. She took the phone the way a barista takes a credit card—transactional.

"Everything okay?" Lola asked.

"Yeah. May have to wait a few days before they can cremate him."

"What's cremate?" Chicho asked.

"Nothing, sweetie," Cat said. "Let's put on your trunks and head out to the beach."

"Yes!" Chicho yelled and ran upstairs, followed by Cat.

"Are you gonna stay?" Lola asked. "Or are you planning to return once the mortuary is ready?"

He shrugged. "Don't know, to be honest. This is a rare downtime for me."

"Cat will take care of anything that comes up. You don't have to feel like you need to stay."

They walked out together. "I'm actually sort of enjoying being back, believe it or not."

"Well, of course you would. I'm here, you dork."

He grinned. "I'm sorry. For not keeping in touch."

"We were never your enemy, Leo."

"I know. But the way I left... I know I burnt bridges. And there was no way to explain it. But you'd been a friend for so long. I should've done something."

She put up her hand. He high-fived her. "Never too late to fix what went wrong." She held his hand. "Or I can drop you right now."

"Fix is better."

So many people in his life kissed up to him in some of the most creative ways, and here were Lola and even Cat. They didn't give a rip. Maybe that's what he needed.

"I saw Billy this morning," he said, recalling another classmate.

Lola's face hardened. "Is that right?"

He studied her face. "Yeah, he said he'd heard I was in town. I assumed it was you or Cat who told him."

She smiled coldly. "Not me, and I can guarantee you that Cat has not been in touch with him."

He needed to peel that one. Clearly, there was no friendship there. Why? Also, if not them, then how did he find out? Roberto?

"You want to join us?" Cat asked as she walked outside with Chicho in tow.

She wore a sun hat that had seen better days. An oversized t-shirt stamped with a band from two decades ago covered what must've been a swimsuit. And her sandals were so large that they may have been his father's. Even so, she looked like sunlight captured in a drop of rain.

"Yeah, sure," he said. He hadn't seen that stretch of the beach in forever.

"Can we take your spaceship there?" Chicho asked, pulling Leo out of his thoughts.

"Probably best we walk it this time," he said.

Chicho held a Superman and Spiderman toy in each hand. He was animated and spoke like a kid who'd been raised on good coffee.

They took the well-worn path from the backyard that took them directly to the sand. Although half the path was relatively easy to traverse, the rest of the path was rough terrain. If he really wanted to build out a resort here, he'd have to do major grading.

"What the...?" Lola said as she stared at something to the side. "Someone took it down again."

Leo walked up to her and glanced at a makeshift fence that had been pushed down to the ground.

"Who's doing this?" Cat asked. "I mean... it's a flimsy gate, but why would anyone not respect the property line and destroy someone else's gate?"

Leo knelt and studied the rotting wood posts that had been kicked down. "Has this happened before?"

Cat grabbed one post and pulled up. "Yes, it happens almost as often as we come here. We haven't been here in a while, but—ouch!" She let go of the post and looked at her palm.

"Splinter?" Lola asked.

"Yeah," she said as she tried to pick it out.

While she did that, he approached the fencing that lay on the ground.

"Leo, don't get your manicured fingers all dirty," Cat said.

Leo eyed her, then turned back to the fence. He lifted the post using the metal wiring that held the post to the fencing and put it back in its barely-there-hole. He adjusted it on both sides until it seemed reasonably sturdy.

"Can't get that one," Cat said as both she and Lola studied her palm, heads conjoined, focused on a tiny shard of wood.

Leo stepped in. "Let me try," he said.

They both glanced at him.

"Gimme," he said, and she complied.

He studied the hand that at one time he had memorized its curves and patterns. He refocused on the skin and, with one hand, squeezed such that it caused the skin to swell and the barely visible splinter to lift. Then with the other hand, he slid a bit of his index finger's nail beneath it and then clamped it with his thumb's nail. He pulled.

"There," he said.

Cat and Lola studied her palm.

"Nice," Lola said.

"Thanks," Cat said.

"Yeah, benefits of manicured nails," he said and walked off.

Lola chuckled.

Cat coughed, "Smartass."

Chapter Twenty-Three

Catalina

Francisco played in the sand with his toys, and God bless Lola, she sat with him the entire time, allowing Cat to get a bit of a breather. For the past week, she'd been constantly 'on,' with naps here and there, but no real rest. She needed this. The late morning sun eliminated the overcast, and a comfortable breeze danced through the bay. She was spent physically and emotionally. So much so fast. Of course, she'd known Lionel senior would pass. She'd been ready for months and had, in some ways, felt relieved that the man would no longer be in pain. It was so hard to see a man who was as strong as him deteriorate the way he had.

And then, of course, there was Leo. So many times, she'd envisioned what she'd tell him if he ever reached out. And maybe, in some way, she got her point across the day before. But, truth be told, she had hoped he'd be devastated by her words. Instead, he took it, absorbed it, and moved on.

How did he do that? How was he able to go on and pretend like he hadn't left a trail of debris behind him? Like everyone else just had to move on and live life.

As if...

She glanced at Leo. In an effortless move, he popped off his shoes, slid off his socks, and rolled up his pants.

He pulled out his camera and walked around, taking pictures, like a tourist. Like he'd never seen this area before.

She eyed his shoes, quickly checked out the brand, then looked up the price on her phone.

Her phone almost fell out of her hand. Who in their right mind spent $1,800 on a pair of butt-ugly shoes and then got them all scuffed up in sand? Some silly Italian hotshot or rapper designer created it, so all those who didn't know how to burn their money bought them.

What she could do if she had two grand... Seemed crazy when she thought of it. When she married Rafael, she was in the lap of financial luxury. He showered her with gifts. Not once did she feel like she lacked. She had access to everything. What she learned quickly was that the barter with the devil meant giving up her freedom, peace, and safety.

Leo walked off to the other end of the beach, taking more pictures. What was he up to? Unlike the rest of Fortuny Bay's beach, this piece was blocked off by boulders on both north and south ends. For the more adventurous types, it wasn't hard to traverse those boulders, but most people stuck to the main beach.

Who was she kidding? Hardly anyone went to the beach. Only the younger people who were still in middle school or high school went to the beach. Most townies worked in the dilapidated fishing community until they died. Or they moved. Like her parents. And Leo.

She got to her feet and joined him. "What are you doing?"

He snapped another picture. "Just... you know."

"No, I don't. It's not like you haven't been here."

He turned to her. "Do you know if my parents' property extends to the beach?"

She frowned. "No clue. He never..." but hesitated, recalling Lionel senior's words.

"What was that?" he asked. "You got a look on your face."

She shook her head. "Maybe it's nothing, but you know how we saw the fence that was down. Well, I said it because he used to say it. Your dad would say people must respect property lines. I assumed they were county lines, not personal property lines. But now I wonder if he was being literal."

"Interesting," he said, and rubbed his jaw.

"But I doubt the beach would be part of the property. Usually, the beaches are state-owned."

"Yeah, I'm sure you're right."

They walked back to the towels. She didn't like that look on his face. He was calculating how much he could sell it for if all this land was also included. Maybe her time here with Chicho was limited, after all.

She slumped on the towel, a bit deflated. He sat near her and leaned back.

"Nice day," he said, but sounded more like someone who was appraising the weather, not enjoying it.

"What did Roberto want?" she asked.

He snapped out of his calculating state. "Just gave me a rundown on what will still need to happen before the cremation. Looks like it'll take a few days still. Maybe a week."

"Not surprising."

"I may head back up today. I'll return when the funeral home is ready to place his ashes. Will you be okay to deal with details until then?" he asked.

She glared at him. "I've been taking care of everything for your father for three years. I'll be fine. Thanks for the concern."

He winced. "Okay, that wasn't an insult. Even though it insulted you. Just trying to be... available."

"A bit late, no?"

"Look, I think it's high time that you and I get into a ring and you go to town on me or get off it once and for all. I am not your enemy."

She scoffed and turned away.

"I am not, okay. I want to help, and I will help."

"And once you're back in your world, this place will be just a line item on your list of assets. Some financial advisor will sell this place without batting an eye. And this place will forever be forgotten. Mister

Top Thirty Under Thirty will go on with his glamorous life, while the rest of this town will be a memory that used to be something but is now nothing."

He shifted to face her more directly. "You don't know anything about me."

"Here's what I know. You are that guy that made me a promise and then broke it in the span of thirty days."

He blinked.

"So whatever you say has probably a shelf life of thirty days."

He swallowed. "Like I said, you don't know me."

"Fine. How long was the longest relationship you've had in the last ten years?"

He didn't respond.

"You live for now—right now. So the concept of a promise or a commitment is not something that runs in your blood. I mean, look at the companies that you've built. You've built two, and what was your long-term plan?"

He stared at her. "The exit strategy was to be acquired," he said, but his voice was low.

"You are a flipper. Build, sell, move on. So forgive me if what you said about this place, this home, does not feel like it's a long-term promise. And when you say you want to help, thank you, but I got this."

She held his gaze. She hated saying what she had, but it needed to be said. Because she could not take chances and allow herself to hope only to be dropped like she had been before. Last time he dumped her, she was on her own. This time, Francisco counted on her.

Her phone rang. She pulled it out of the bag. Roberto was calling again.

"Hi Roberto," she said as she opened the call on speakerphone. "Looking for Leo?"

"Yes, please."

"He's right here. Is it private? I have you on speaker."

"No, not at all. Good for you both to hear it."

"Go on," Leo said.

"Some good news," Roberto said. "The medical examiner and county fast-tracked your father's death certificate. You may have it as early as tomorrow. This is really unprecedented. We typically run at a different pace."

"Wow," Leo said. "That's good news. But how did that happen?"

"It seems that Doña Adela Roca put a call in."

Leo's eyes widened. "Is that right?"

"Yes. She apparently told them to expedite it for her friend."

Silence.

Cat stared at him. "What's that about?" she asked, almost appalled.

"She joined me this morning at the cafe. I think she likes me."

"She must," Roberto said.

Cat stopped listening. Doña Adela didn't like anyone except herself.

[illegible]

[illegible]
[illegible]
[illegible]
[illegible]
[illegible]

[illegible]
[illegible]
[illegible]

[illegible]

Chapter Twenty-Four

Leo

Leo left them at the beach when he received the email that the refrigerator delivery truck would arrive within thirty minutes. He sped back to the house, the conversation with Cat still in his mind.

He wanted to tell her off. He wanted to push back on everything she brought up. But the one thing that he couldn't deny was that she was right. She was. How could he defend his actions other than with the truth? He hadn't told her he had applied to another university—his backup plan. When he got denied from Stanford, he'd seen it on her face—she was disappointed. He had not lived up to the expectations. And his dad's words nailed exactly how he felt. He was a loser.

He knew he had to venture off on his own. He would show them all. And once he had graduated and had landed an amazing job, he'd come back to her, to show her he was not defined by those who said no to him.

But his plan changed before the first year ended. He got noticed.

He got funding. Leo became rich before he turned twenty. And with the money came the lifestyle. He was free to do what he wanted, how he wanted, with whomever he wanted.

Leo never looked back. He wanted out of the constraints of the past. He wanted to live life. He wanted to be that guy that escaped the small town and made it. And made it he had.

He reached the house, and within a few minutes, the delivery truck arrived. Two guys hopped out of the truck and evaluated the house.

Leo showed them the challenge. "The doorway is narrow," Leo said.

"We'll have to take the door out," one of them said unhappily.

"And then I want to get rid of the old fridge."

"We don't do that, sir. Even the door—"

Leo pulled out his money clip and peeled off four hundred dollars and split it between them. "I really need your help with this."

A new motivation entered the eyes of the delivery guys.

"We're on it," one said.

"I'll get the door; you unload the fridge," the other said to his partner.

They worked quickly and with purpose. By the time Cat and Chicho came back, the three of them were finishing ice-cold bottles of beer.

"What's going on?" Cat asked as she and Chicho entered the kitchen.

"All done. What do you think?" Leo asked.

She studied the stainless steel refrigerator. It was larger, but not unreasonably so. She ran her fingers across the water dispenser.

"Does this work?" she asked, looking hopeful.

"Yes, Ma'am," one guy said. Leo had given them another $200 to get that installed.

She opened the door. The bright light from inside the refrigerator illuminated her.

"Mommy, this is amazing!" Chicho said. "Let's go buy more apples!"

The guys chuckled.

"Happy wife, happy life," one of them said.

She faced him, her face red. "Not his wife."

"Sorry," the guy said, embarrassed.

"Alright, guys. Let's get you to your next delivery. Thanks again," Leo said.

"Thank you, Mister."

Leo walked them to the kitchen door and watched them run to the truck, high-fiving each other.

"It's a nice fridge," she said.

"Yeah, a bit better than the avocado green one." He scanned around. "Where's Lola?"

"She went back to her parents." She picked up Chicho and placed him on her hip. "Let's take a nap. What do you say?"

"Are you tired, Mommy?"

"Yeah, I'm tired."

They left the kitchen and walked up the stairs. He studied her in awe. *Cat's a pretty good mom.* He watched her still-toned calves flex with each step. *A very attractive mom.*

He blinked. *Stop it.*

He returned to his father's study and walked around the room. Books on top of books shoved in the shelves. Hundreds of copies of National Geographic. Boxes of receipts and other paperwork. And then there was his desk.

He sat in his father's chair. The squeak that it produced was like the switch of a time machine. Immediately, he recalled the times that he'd lain on the floor reading a book while his father did the accounting or taxes of his clients. He didn't believe his father was a certified accountant, but he had a lot of clients. Both the fishermen and even the support businesses. And when it was tax season, the smallest noise was the equivalent to a tsunami warning for him.

The man was always distant. Leo couldn't ever recall his father embracing him or telling him he loved Leo. No, that's not who he was. He was analytical. Debits and credits were how he saw the world. Pros and cons. Winners and losers.

And who really lost in the end? Leo or his father, who passed away, basically broke?

Stop being an ass, Leo.

He recalled the family photo in Disneyland. Clearly, his father hadn't always been distant. He ran his hand across the desk. Leo had never appreciated the beauty and craftsmanship of it. He wondered if it was from France or from Spain.

His father's ancient PC sat on the left side of the desk. Dust had settled on the keyboard. The desk blotter was clean, except for one piece of paper that had some names and numbers on it. To the far side was an oversized notepad, the type that accountants used for tracking ledgers.

Leo pulled the pad and opened it. He frowned. These were not debits and credits. The columns were simple. One had the date. The other said yes or no. The dates went back to over fifteen years ago. Page after page of small print writing. Most of the dates said no, and a random few said yes.

"Are you looking for anything specific?"

Leo jumped at Cat's voice. He put his hand on his heart.

She laughed. "Sorry. Didn't mean to scare you."

"I may need to change my pants," he said, which caused her to smile. He liked it when she smiled.

She walked in and looked over his shoulder. "Oh, that."

"What was he tracking?" he asked.

"Honestly, no clue. He stopped doing that some three months ago. He used to take a walk at night alone. He wouldn't allow me to walk with him. Instead, I'd wait outside and watch him walk toward the edge where he could see the ocean. He'd sit on a chair he used to have there and watch the horizon for a good thirty minutes. Sometimes more. Then he'd waltz back in and put in a yes or a no."

Leo stared at her. "That's just weird."

She shrugged. "Maybe. Whatever it was, it was important to him. I wondered if he was meditating or praying. Sometimes, when he returned, he'd go into his conspiracy rants from the moon landing to theories about this town's dirty secrets and how everyone was in on it. His words, not mine."

"A bit paranoid, no?"

She shrugged. "Maybe a bit. From my perspective, one thing's for sure, they are all of one mind in Fortuny Bay. No one goes off the reservation around here."

Leo returned his attention back to the ledger. What could this have been about?

"Hungry?" she asked.

He looked up. "Starved."

"Come on. Let's see what we can slap together."

Chapter Twenty-Five

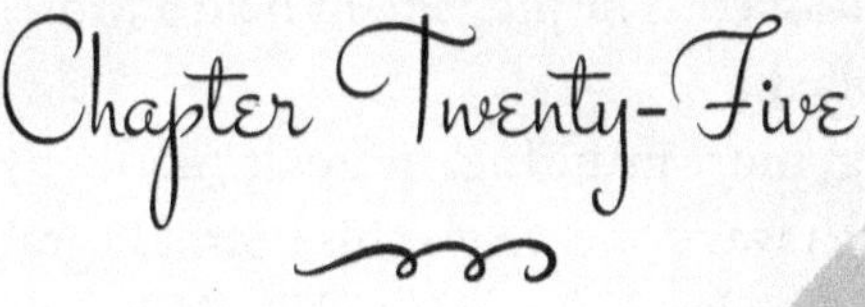

Leo

While the sourdough bread toasted, Leo sliced the tomatoes, and Cat assembled the bits and pieces she needed for the ham and turkey sandwiches. When the toaster rang, she dropped the slices on the plates. She made a concoction including dijon mustard, mayo, and some other things he did not recognize. By the time she was done, it was reddish. She showed him the dressing. He nodded. After she lathered the bread, she lifted each pile and sandwiched it between the toasted breads, then sliced diagonally. He was certain at some point she'd worked as a short-order cook. He pulled a bottle of beer, showed it to her. She shook her head. He popped the cap before he joined her at the table.

She lowered her head, whispered something, then said, "Amen."

There she was again. Getting all religious. This had to be new.

He decided to not question her and instead lifted his sandwich and bit into it. As he chewed, he realized that either this was the best sandwich he'd had in a very long time, or he was starving, in which case cardboard would taste as good as Belgian chocolate.

"Mmm," he said.

"Yeah," she agreed.

He took a long drag from his bottle, emptying a good third.

"Thirsty?" she asked. The judgement held a Moses-like tone to it.

"Very," he replied.

More chewing, more grunting, more drinking. By the time the first half of his sandwich was done, so was his beer. He grabbed another one.

She studied him as he took a swig. "What?" he asked.

She hesitated. "Nothing." Cat turned her attention back to her food.

The look on her face reminded him of Anna. Concern? Accusation?

"When did your husband pass away?" he asked.

She came to an abrupt stop, then glanced up at him for a moment. Then she dropped her eyes to her food. "Almost four years ago. November. On Thanksgiving."

A long pause.

"Francisco was…"

"Just over a year old."

"So he never knew his dad."

She shook her head. "No."

He took a sip. "Mind if I dig a bit?"

She drank some water. "I'll tell you when you hit the un-digable ground."

"Fair enough." He set his bottle down and picked up the second half of his sandwich. "How'd you two meet?"

She grinned. "At school."

He straightened. "What? Who?"

She took another sip of water. "Raf Marceli."

His expression must have betrayed him because her face tightened. "Raf, the Jerky Marceli? Are you serious?"

Her jaw set, and her eyes hardened. "Yes."

"But, he was always such a bully. Class A jerk."

"Unlike you, right?"

He hesitated. A few seconds ticked by. "At least I wasn't a bully."

"But you concede that you're a jerk."

He took another bite of his sandwich. "Maybe, a bit," he said between chews.

They finished their sandwiches and drinks in silence. Leo rose, grabbed her plate and his, and took them to the sink. He washed the dishes, all the while thinking of Raf. Raf was a brute. Two years older than them. Five years more immature. Why would she have gone for him? The family did have money. He received a nice Beamer when he turned sixteen. Was it the money? If so, what happened? Why was she broke now?

He'd met a lot of people who showed wealth, but it was all credit cards and debt and pretense. Underneath it all, they were not only poor, they were in debt up to their ears.

He needed to know. "How did you two get together?"

She seemed to consider where to start. "After you left, I had to reconsider my school options. Do I go to where we'd planned to attend together, or do I reset and go to a school I wanted to go to?"

He recalled receiving the rejection letter and relived the emotions he felt. He could no longer use the attack lines he'd prepared for his dad. Leo felt embarrassed. Maybe because his dad had been right. He was, after all, like everyone else in this town—average. And on some level, he thought she saw him differently. Almost as if he was not who she thought he was.

So, when Chris, his gaming buddy who later would become his partner, told him about the college he was going to attend, he applied as his hedge. That school had already said yes and had even offered a partial scholarship when Stanford said no. He took the exit ticket and left everyone behind.

He remembered his empty words to her after he told her he was leaving: "Maybe you can transfer next year."

Leo cringed at the memory of her reaction to that statement. He should've been transparent with her. She was right. He had been a jerk.

"Turned out I was too late to try for other schools," she continued. "So, I got a job at the campus bookstore, and in walked Raf. He was on his last year—or so he claimed." She smiled. "I think he attended to meet girls."

Leo's eyes widened as he sat back down. This guy was a prize.

"We talked. He charmed me. More accurately, I allowed myself to be charmed. It was very easy. And I admit, their lifestyle was a draw. Things just happened. My parents fell in love with him, and so did I, eventually. Those were hopeful days." Her eyes drifted to another place, another time. He decided to leave it there.

"I had no idea," he said, unsure of what else he should say.

"Yeah, well... typically, when you cut off everyone, by definition, you will not have any idea of what they've been up to."

He didn't know what to say to that either.

"Coffee?" she offered, successfully killing the awkward moment.

"Yeah, that'd be great."

"Don't get too excited. This isn't one of your organic, coffee-beans-out-of-the-poop-of-a-monkey type of drink. It's instant."

"Desperate times... I'll have to get one shipped here."

She took a deep breath, and her shoulders sagged.

"It's just a coffee machine," he said.

She smirked. "It's odd. When we don't have, we hope for break-throughs. When we get, we miss the innocence of the past. I look at the refrigerator, and it reminds me of some constructions I've seen in New York and other cities. The old gets demolished, and the new gets propped up. But to the left and the right are still the crappy old buildings."

"Until they are gone, too," he said. "Gentrification."

"It sounds so noble. Gentrification... but it really means out with the old, in with the new."

They both stared at the refrigerator. To the right, an oven that Columbus probably brought with him. To the left was a Formica countertop whose plastic top was peeling.

He turned to her. "Where's that coffee?"

"Right. Let's enjoy it before you gentrify the coffee, too."

"Just a matter of time," he said.

She mixed the crystals with hot water, then put the dry creamer and sugar on the table. She added stale butter cookies from a tin can that had been in the pantry for at least two presidents.

"Wow, this is totally—"

"Beneath you?" she asked.

"No, charming in its own weird way."

They sipped and dipped the cookies.

After a few moments, he asked what had been on his mind. "How did Raf pass?"

She bore into his eyes. "Boating accident. Went sailing when he shouldn't have. And that's where I stop."

He respected her boundary. But his mind raced, wondering if Raf had cut her and Chicho off financially. Or was it some sort of insurance hold up? After four years, he didn't think so.

"What'cha guys doing?" Chicho asked as he dragged himself down the stairs.

"Waiting for you, little buddy. Hungry?" she asked.

"Mac and cheese?" he asked.

"You got it." She kissed the top of his head and went to work.

She was a wonderful mom. Chicho was very lucky to have her. And he supposed she'd been lucky that his father had taken her in. What would've happened to them, he wondered, if not for his father's hospitality? He wasn't sure, but didn't want to think of that. They were fine. And he'd make sure they were fine, too. He chuckled. The first time he and his father agreed on something... it was bound to be about Cat.

[illegible]

Chapter Twenty-Six

Catalina

Chicho was finishing up his meal when Leo ran downstairs, his hair wet and skin damp from the quick shower he'd just taken.

"I'm gonna take off and head back home," he said. "Once Roberto gives you the details, can you let me know?"

"Are you sure?" Cat asked. She checked herself. Why was she feeling a bit of sadness? If he wanted to go, he could go.

"Where is your home?" Chicho asked.

Leo sat down next to Chicho. "It's a place called San Jose. I have to drive about three hours to get there."

His eyes went wide. "That's so far!"

"Not too bad."

Chicho shoveled a spoonful of cheesy pasta in his mouth, chewed, then said, "This is my house."

"Chicho, this is—" she started to correct but was stopped by Leo.

"I like your house."

"It's your house, too," Chicho said. "I've seen your room. Your bed is enormous."

"True."

"So why don't you stay in this house?"

Leo rose. "Next time I visit, I will. Right now, I have to take care of some work in my other house."

"Okay, I'll come with you," Chicho said, and hopped off the chair. "I need my Spiderman and my pencils."

"Hold it there, big guy," Cat said. "We're not going anywhere." How she wished she could take him far away from here.

"It's okay, Mommy, I'll go."

Leo smiled. "Next time, we can all go together."

Chicho didn't look happy. "You promise to come back?"

"Yes, of course."

The boy seemed satisfied. "Okay. Deal."

Leo took a deep breath. "Okay, I better take off."

"One problem," Cat said. "I don't have your number."

He grinned. "So, this is how you get my digits."

She glared at him. "Just give me the info and leave."

Just as he finished adding his contact information, the phone rang in his hand. He quickly handed it to her.

"Who now?" she asked, then glanced at the screen. "Roberto again. It'll be for you."

She handed him the phone, and he answered it and placed it on speakerphone. "Hi Roberto," he said.

"Oh, hi Leo. Wasn't expecting you to answer it. Glad you did. Is Catalina there also?"

"Yup, right here. Got you on speakerphone."

"Very good. Can you both come to my office tomorrow morning at 9 am?"

A hesitation. He exchanged looks with her. "I planned to return to San Jose today. Is this something that can wait? Or something that Cat might address on my behalf?"

"Well, I need both of you there, as it concerns both of you. It's about your dad's will. I just received a FedEx package. It seems he had another attorney in San Luis Obispo who prepared his estate plans."

"SLO?" Cat asked, then snapped her finger. "Is his name something like Martini?"

"Close. Maroutian. How did you know?"

"Lionel received a package months back. Like six or seven months ago. He then asked me to have it shipped back. I saw the name and thought it was unique."

Leo stared at her, then returned his attention to the phone. "So, this is about a will he wrote?"

"Correct. And the instructions I received from the law firm were to find you—which thankfully is done—and to have you and miss Catalina Alonzo there."

"Me?" she asked.

"Yes. I've been asked to have you both present. Mr. Maroutian will join us via a videoconference."

Both Cat and Leo frowned.

"Well," Leo finally said. "I guess I won't leave after all. We'll be there at nine."

"Excellent. See you then."

The phone connection ended.

"Awesome," Chicho said. "You get to sleep here tonight."

Leo turned to him. "Yeah, I guess so."

"We'll make popcorn and watch cartoons."

Leo turned to Cat. She could see that he was searching her eyes for some clarity. But she was more confused than he was.

"Leo, I have no idea what this is all about."

He shrugged. "Don't sweat it. We'll know tomorrow." He hesitated. "Are you okay with me staying here?"

She smirked. "I trust you." She turned and walked away.

"But can I trust you?" he asked.

She eyed him. She could not see her own face. But his changing expression and look of fear confirmed what she hoped to convey. Stop him dead in his tracks from thinking he could flirt with her.

[illegible]

[illegible]

[illegible]

[illegible]
[illegible]
[illegible]

[illegible]

[illegible]
[illegible]

[illegible]

[illegible]

[illegible]
[illegible]
[illegible]

[illegible]

[illegible]
[illegible]

Chapter Twenty-Seven

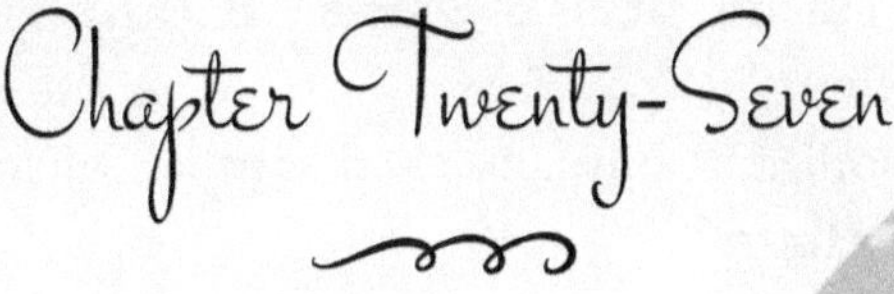

Leo

Leo convinced Cat and Lola to go out to an early dinner instead of cooking. He loved the stuff she'd prepared so far. Admittedly, he even enjoyed the hot dogs she made. But he wanted to check out the town a bit more. He wanted to get a better feel for the "night life," if there was any. Also, if he was going to drop serious money to build a resort, he would have to consider one or two restaurants on site. If there were excellent dining options already in town, he'd have to figure out the niche he'd need to fill.

"Let's check out Harvey's Barbecue," Lola said. "We haven't tried it."

"Because it's expensive," Cat said.

"He's paying," Lola said.

"I am. Let's go. Where's Chicho?"

"Right here," a tiny voice said from directly next to him.

"Excellent. Let's go."

Twenty minutes later, he was parking his truck on the street. No valet, so not high-end. He glanced at the flickering neon lights and decided he would not have much competition if he added an upscale restaurant to his resort.

They walked into the restaurant, and the smell of hearty barbecue sauce and charred meat hit his senses immediately. It smelled great, but he could almost cut the smell of grease from the atmosphere with a knife.

The hostess smiled at him and then scanned the others. Her smile faltered. "Table for four?"

"Yes," Leo said.

He studied the faces in the restaurant. A handful appeared to be staring at them.

Did they recognize him or was it something else?

He spotted Billy and was about to wave, but the look on the deputy's face stopped him. Billy was staring directly at Cat.

"Can we go?" Cat asked, her voice low.

He turned to her. "Why?" He saw her eyes were bloodshot.

"Please?" she whispered.

"Absolutely," he said, and immediately ushered them out of the restaurant.

"Where are we going?" Chicho asked.

"We're going to take a short drive to somewhere else," he said.

"Hold on," Cat said. "Lola, buckle him in, please. I need to say something to Leo."

Lola nodded and lifted Chicho into the truck.

"What's going on?"

She bit the inside of her cheek, not able to hold eye contact with him. "Can we just go back home?"

"You don't want to go to the nearest town and—?"

"We can't." In her expression, he saw there was more to it than she was willing to explain. He wouldn't push her.

"Got it. Let's go home."

Once they were in the car, he dialed a number.

"Hello, Mr. Moncrieff. How can I help you?"

"I'm sending over my address. Please confirm receipt."

After a few seconds, the operator said, "In Fortuny Bay?"

"Yes."

"Very well. What can I do for you?"

"I need expedited delivery of real tasty barbecue, but not from Fortuny Bay. Two full slabs, a couple of whole chickens, two pounds of steak, and a bunch of sides."

"Corn on the cob!" Chicho yelled.

"Corn on the cob, beans, surprise me. But I need the food in hand in the next hour. All delivery options approved."

"Including helicopter?" she asked.

"Approved."

"Very well. Anything else?"

"Two bottles of wine. Something ridiculously good."

"Understood."

"One hour," Leo reminded.

"You got it."

He tapped the screen and cut the connection. "Awesome. Who needs Harvey's?" He turned to face Cat. She was staring at him, mouth open.

"Did you just tell them to deliver our dinner by helicopter?" Lola asked from the back row.

"Yes...?" he said hesitantly.

"Was that necessary?" Cat asked. "We could've gotten pizza, or I could've made pasta."

"I want ribs," Chicho said.

"The kid wants ribs," Leo said. "And... yeah. I'm really hungry."

Cat shook her head. "This feels wrong, but... ribs do sound good." She grinned. Just then, the door to Harvey's Barbecue opened, and a couple that Leo didn't recognize stepped out and stared at them.

Cat put her hand on his arm. "Let's go, please."

He thought they were staring at the truck. For some reason, she felt otherwise. He didn't argue.

Three hours later, they had all stuffed themselves to the max and were sitting on the back porch. A helicopter was not required in the end.

Instead, a motorcycle delivered the meal. Only six minutes late, but who was counting?

As they waited and entertained Chicho, Leo burst at the seams, wanting to know what in the world was going on with Cat in that restaurant. What was the story there? But he controlled himself, knowing that at some point, Chicho would go to sleep.

"Good night," Leo said when Lola and Chicho went up to his room. "She's awesome with him," he said to a lost in thought Cat.

She snapped out of it. "Lo? She's my angel. She's been a rock. I'm going to miss her when she goes back to Pismo."

He rose. "Come on, let's take a walk."

She stared at him.

"It's just a walk."

"But you're going to ask questions."

"Yup," he said and held her eyes.

She nodded and rose. They walked in silence, heading toward the same spot that Leo had parked on the first night.

"What was that all about at the restaurant?" he asked.

She kicked a stone into the darkness. "Didn't you see how they were staring at me?"

They came to a stop and gazed at the moonlit ocean.

He wasn't sure exactly what she was talking about or if they were staring at her, but he went with it. "Why you?" he asked.

"Because there are some people in this town who liked Raf more than me. And many of the same felt that I married Raf for his money."

He glance at her.

"Clearly, as you can tell, I am not bathing in his wealth."

"What happened? Was he broke?"

"Oh no. That family is wealthier than I could've imagined."

He scratched his head. "Then what? Was there a prenup or something?"

She shoved her hands into her front pockets. "Not one that I signed. But somehow, one was produced after his death."

His eyes grew wide. "You're kidding?"

"Nope. It's been a long and hard journey." She squinted toward the ocean. "What's that?"

He faced the water and immediately saw what she was studying. A silhouette of a decent-sized ship. And pulling away from it, a smaller boat, with one beam of light up front. It was quite a distance away, but he could make it out clearly. It was not a trick of the eye. There were two objects in the ocean.

"What are they doing?" he asked.

She hesitated. "Not sure."

"Have you ever seen this before?"

"Never."

Fishing boats were not uncommon. But what he was witnessing did not look like fishing activity. Also, a hundred yards away from the sandy beach was never a fishing destination. This made little sense. He started walking toward the shore, but she held him back.

"What do you think you're doing?" she asked.

"Gonna check it out."

"Please don't. You don't know what they're doing and who they are. We're alone here. And I have a five-year-old."

He wanted to explain that he'd be safe and he'd be fine. But the look in her eyes told him she was not ready to hear that.

"Okay," he said. "Let's get back home."

When they entered the house, Lola gingerly walked down the stairs. "He's out."

"Thank you," Cat said, then hugged her friend. "Go home and please be safe."

"Will do." She hugged Leo. "Thanks for dinner, and that flipping wine was indeed ridiculous."

He grinned. "I'll get you more."

"Not gonna argue with you."

Once Lola left, Leo watched Cat check each window's lock. Then each door. And then the windows one more time.

What is she so scared of?

Chapter Twenty-Eight

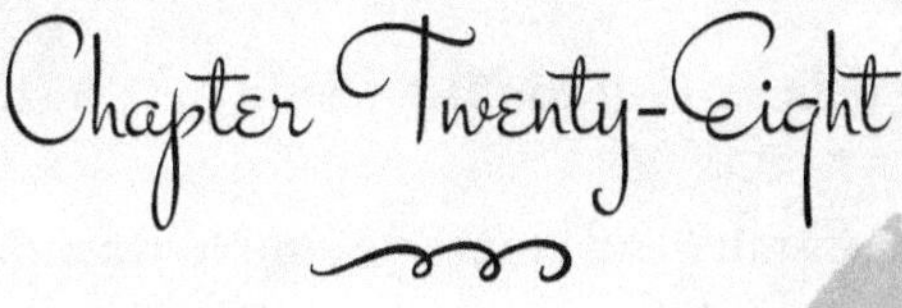

Leo

Against his better judgement, Leo agreed to walk to Roberto's office. Cat insisted that driving was not healthy when a twenty-minute walk was an option. Also, she wanted Chicho to get some physical activity in.

A coastal blanket of fog and mist covered the town. It was a bit chilly, but not too bad. He wore shorts, not by choice, but because he was on his last change of clothes. Either way, today, he'd have to head home, buy clothes here, or have some couriered over.

"I miss him," Chicho said.

"Me too," Cat said.

Chicho looked at Leo, waiting for confirmation. Instead, he just smiled at the kid and hoped that gesture was a good enough deflection.

His phone rang. It was Anna.

"Mornin'," he said, "What's up?"

"Sophie got information on the property. Is this a good time?"

He sped up to cross the street. "Send me the details, and I'll call you back in an hour or so. Meeting with my father's attorney."

"Everything okay?"

He shrugged. Not that she'd see. "I suppose."

Cat came to a stop in front of a bland two-story building. She pointed upward.

"Anyway, we're here. Call you later. Send me the stuff."

"Will do."

They walked upstairs and entered a simple reception area. A couch that would've been stylish in the '90s waited for them.

"I'll tell him you're here," the receptionist said. She showed no emotion. A robot at best.

After she buzzed him, she nodded, then hung up. "You can go in. I'll keep the young man entertained."

"Thanks," Cat said. She followed Leo through the double door into Roberto's office.

Roberto was already walking toward the door when they walked in. "Good morning. Perfect timing. Do you want coffee, water, tea?"

After they each received their drink of choice, they sat at the small, four-person circular table. Speakerphone in the center, laptop on the fourth spot. A pop-up screen alerted them that the host would open the meeting soon.

"Do you know this man?" Leo asked.

"Maroutian? No. I looked him up, and he's been at it for a while. Seems well—"

The screen changed, and an older man appeared on the screen. Roberto fumbled with the computer, until Leo tapped two keys, and both the camera and speaker were engaged.

"Good morning," Mr. Maroutian said. His voice was firm but friendly. His eyes were downcast, with bushy grey eyebrows. His mane of wiry salt and pepper hair gave him more of a professorial look than of a bloodsucking lawyer.

They quickly introduced themselves and then paused for Maroutian to speak.

"Let's get into it," he said. "I know Mr. Moncrieff is a busy man, and Ms. Alonzo has her hands full with Francisco."

Leo smiled. The man had either done his homework or knew a lot about them from his father.

"Mr. Chaparral, first, thank you for finding Mr. Moncrieff the younger. I know his father did not have high hopes, but seeing him here gives me great pleasure. As you will see, I am also the executor. My client, Mr. Moncrieff, had a living trust and will. Now, Mr. Chaparral, please open the sealed envelope. I have a copy here as well."

Roberto opened the envelope and appeared to be scanning the contents quickly. His eyes widened.

Maroutian slid on his spectacles and read the preamble, then moved on to the meat. "The totality of Mr. Lionel Moncrieff's estate includes his home, *Casa Moncrieff,* at 2307 Cove Place in Fortuny Bay, California. His savings and checking account with American Bank, valued at $122,911. His mutual funds with Fidelity, valued at $73,904. And all material belongings inside the home, garage, and barn on said property." He looked up. "Those items were not valued." He lowered his glasses. "All these assets were transferred to the trust and will therefore avoid probate. Questions?"

Leo shook his head. "Seems accurate."

Maroutian cleared his throat. "I, Lionel Moncrieff, being of sound mind, leave the entirety of my estate to Miss Catalina Alonzo."

"What?!" she yelled and rose, nearly knocking her chair backward.

Leo's face went numb.

His left eye twitched.

The world went silent, muffled, like when he swam in his pool. His heavy heartbeat replaced the rhythmic beat of the speakers.

He should've known. Still, he did not think his father would go this low. The house where his mom gave birth to him. The house that was a home until the day his mom passed away. The home that had been in the family for generations.

So be it, he thought.

He rose and walked out of the office, uninterested in anything that Cat and the lawyers had to say.

Leo walked through the waiting room.

"Leo, please wait," Cat said. Or at least that's what he thought she said. He was not interested.

Chicho rose and called out his name, but Leo didn't respond to him either. He didn't look at him, and he didn't slow down.

Leo calmly, but with iron-clad focus, walked down the stairs and wandered outdoor. He stopped, closed his eyes, and took a deep breath. As he exhaled, he opened his eyes again.

"Well played, old man," he whispered.

He shouldn't have been surprised that his father did this. He chuckled. The vindictive man even asked for both attorneys to find him. Why? Clearly, to give him the finger from the grave.

His father sure nailed it. A perfect 10, declared the Russian and French judges.

He searched the storefronts up and down the street. There. The cafe that Billy had taken him to. What was that server's name? Barb, he thought.

He needed something more potent than coffee, but this would have to do for now. Maybe another Nutella-infused croissant would do the trick.

"Hey there," Barb said when he walked in. "Welcome back, Leo." She ushered him to the same table he'd taken before.

"Coffee. Nutella croissant. Double."

She nodded in understanding. "One of those days?"

"You have no idea," he said.

"On it."

How could his father will away what had been his generational right? He had to admit, the lost opportunity for financial gains bothered him too. He had planned a bit too much about what he'd do with that property.

He remembered Anna was going to email him information on the property. Maybe the property was just the home and not the land. He launched his email app, opened the report from Sophie Perez, and grunted.

Twenty flipping acres!

But on the same note, Anna emphasized the word 'However' in red and uppercase. "It is close to impossible to get a resort permit. Nothing, I mean NOTHING, has been approved that is touristy in any way, shape, or form. One option: bribe the city council."

He turned off his phone and set it down. *Screw it and screw them.* He would've brought tremendous revenues to this dead city. But it didn't matter now.

Barb placed his coffee and pastries in front of him, then scooted away.

Was that will binding? Cat said the other attorney got involved six or seven months ago. His father was well into his illness. Was he of a competent mind? What if he had made those changes under duress?

He recalled Adela's words about Cat.

I know that Miss Alonzo was very close to your father. Almost like a daughter.

What if she had talked him into leaving her something? Or everything. What if this was all part of her plan? She knew he was ill. She'd take her time, wait him out and then win him over.

But that's not who she was... or at least that's not the Cat that he knew. Then again, life had a tendency to change people. Sometimes bullies became priests. And sometimes angels fell.

[illegible]

Chapter Twenty-Nine

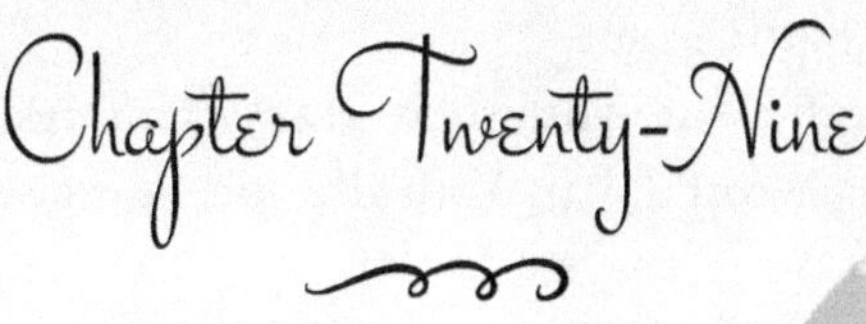

Catalina

Cat wanted to go after Leo, but the attorneys asked her to stay. They explained she needed to understand what it all meant and what had to be done to transfer everything to her name. After the call with Maroutian ended, she rose.

"Before you leave," Roberto said, "let's talk about a few things."

She nodded, then sat back down. Leo was still on her mind. She wanted to call him, but she also didn't want to drop the ball on this generous, unbelievable gift.

"You might consider speaking to a realtor," Roberto said.

"Why would I do that?" she asked. Had he not heard the instructions?

He placed his hand on hers. She wanted to pull it out, but out of respect, she didn't move.

"Taking on a house of that size and that age would be too much for most. But for a single mother with all those other details hovering over

"

her... well, it could be a nightmare. This is an amazing gift, but it could become a money pit as well."

"I have to think about it," she said. Truth be told, she did not want to think about it. She'd been entrusted with a house that had been in the family for well over a century. She'd been given a responsibility, and she needed to just figure it out.

"One thing I can assure you, there are *very* interested people in that house. You could get top dollar. Your life and Francisco's future would be set."

She stared into his eyes. He seemed like he was trying to be helpful, but something about this conversation made her feel dirty.

She rose. "Thank you, Mr. Chaparral. I have to think about all these points."

He rose as well. "Of course. Please contact me and let me know how you'd like to proceed or if you want to consider different scenarios and options."

"I will," she said. She lumbered out of Roberto's office and slid the copy of the will and the note for Leo in her purse. Her head spun with the details, the implications, the expectations, and the fear that went with it.

"Catalina," Roberto called out.

She turned and faced him.

"This is a lot to digest. But... I want you to know that you're not alone. I can help you." He ran his hand through his hair. "I can give you advice, guidance, and identify options that may not be as overwhelming."

She nodded. "Thank you, Roberto. Like I said, I have to think about it and pray about it." Why was he pushing her so much?

"Sure. Yes, you do that. You will call on me, yes? Whatever you decide, let me know."

"Of course. Yeah."

He smiled, looking relieved. "Very good. So long as you remember that you have a friend in me. A confidant."

"Thank you, Roberto. For all you did for Lionel and for me."

He placed a hand on her shoulder and squeezed it. "Be safe."

She did all she could to not shake his hand off her shoulder.

She took Chicho's hand and left the office. This was not happening. Lionel had sometimes thrown comments like, "I'll take care of you two," or "I won't let those people break you." But this... this was not what was supposed to happen.

And now Leo was hurt. Who could blame him?

"What's wrong, Mommy? You look sad."

She lowered herself and cupped his face. "I'm not sad, sweetie. Not really. I'm just a little confused."

"Do you need me to help you?"

Her eyes widened. "Maybe not right now, but thank you for wanting to help me."

He hugged her. "I love you," he said.

She wanted to cry. With all that had gone wrong in her life, this little man had been the blessing she did not deserve. And yet, here he was.

"Let's go home," she said. "I think I need a grilled cheese sandwich."

"Me too. With pickles?"

"Absolutely."

As they walked back, she wondered if this change in her situation— this unexpected tsunami—would finally get her back on track and out of the jam she'd been in for the last three-plus years. As much as she hated to think about it, the fact was that within the next few days, she'd have access to money. She would no longer be poor, on the brink of losing the only thread of hope she had.

She felt her face flush. For some reason, she felt embarrassed. A thief. An outsider—an interloper—who'd come in and taken away someone else's rightful property.

Then again, Lionel wanted her to have it. He entrusted *her* with it. Particularly if she was going to move forward with his request in the will.

But the bigger issue now was Leo. That poor guy had kept away from his dad because he felt his father didn't love him. And now, with this act, he had, in effect, the proof that sealed what he always assumed.

She couldn't believe that Lionel had done that to his own son.

Cat squeezed the bridge of her nose. She wished Leo had sat

through the reading. He would've heard some of the details. Would he have cared? Probably not.

Cat needed to bring Lola up to speed. She texted her.

> You need to come over ASAP

She and Chicho crossed the street toward the house. The phone chimed. It was Lola.

> Is everything okay? Are you hurt?

Cat frowned.

> Just come

The real question was, what would she tell Leo? How could she win his trust? She scoffed. Was he still in town? For all she knew, he was gone, never to come back again.

As they turned the corner, the truck's gleaming surface gave her a portion of the answer. He was still here. For now. She had to make sure she spoke to him before he left town.

Chapter Thirty

Leo

Leo ignored Cat's texts and calls. Instead, he spent the rest of the morning in the cafe reading various white papers from his engineers. He had some brilliant people on his team. He'd have to plan his next move. Step one was to brainstorm. Step two, pull Anna and Chris into his next venture.

His phone chimed again. He nearly blocked her.

Keep it above middle school behavior, Leo.

He had to admit that her reaction during the will reading sounded as shocked as he felt. Maybe she had worked his father but never thought he'd go full bore. Maybe she hoped for a bit of money. But not all of it.

Why was he thinking about this? *Who cares?*

He wanted to act like he didn't care. But he did. Man, this really pissed him off. If his father was in a fit state of mind and he wanted to do this, then so be it. He could accept that. Probably. But... but what if this was more than met the eye?

He left a hefty tip for Barb and left the cafe. He called the only person who could see through the clutter. But Anna was apparently unavailable. He didn't want to bother Chris while he was busy transitioning with Gaming Kings, but he needed to talk to someone.

"Bro," Leo said.

"Sup'? You okay?" Chris asked.

"I just left my father's will reading."

"The will? Good thing he planned ahead, you never want to—"

"He left everything to Cat."

Silence.

"Are you there?" Leo asked.

"Yeah. I'm here. Just… you know… processing it. Are you okay, Dude?"

He paced the sidewalk, probably looking like a madman, but right now, he didn't care.

"I want to be okay. But I'm not. I can't help but think that there's funny business going on here."

"Funny business? As in a fake will?"

"No, I believe that he did it legitimately. But what if he was 'talked' into it? You feel me?"

"Who would've done that?"

"My ex. Cat."

Chris blew out air. "Okay, yeah. Anna told me she's been living in your dad's house." A hesitation. "So you're saying Cat somehow convinced a frail, sick man to change his will?"

"Bingo!"

"You've spent the last three days with her. Any hint that she knew what was coming? Does she come across as the person who would do that?"

He scratched his head, even though there was no itch there. "Not sure. Not enough time to formulate an opinion."

"Nope. I call cap."

"What do you mean?" he asked. "I'm being legit here. I need more time to—"

"No way. You have opinions about people you meet in the first thirty seconds. And most of the time, you're spot on. You read people like their true persona was tattooed on their forehead."

He was right. But this time was different. "I have a past with her, so I'm not at the top of my game. Plus, she probably knows how to speak to me."

"You don't even sound like yourself. And please stop pacing. I can hear your movements, and I'm getting seasick."

He leaned against a wall.

"Take a deep breath," Chris instructed.

He did.

"Now, let's think like a detective. Did she have a motive?"

He nodded. "Yes, she has a very solid motive. She and her son are poor."

"Hmm. Okay. Did she have the means to talk your dad into changing his will?"

"Yes."

"So she has the means and the motive. But was your dad the type of person who could be manipulated?"

He chuckled. "No way. That's the truth. Unless he was senile and unaware of his surroundings. Otherwise, that skill of mine to read people... well, that came from him."

Which is why when his father called him a loser, it had hurt especially hard.

"Then how could he let her get away with it for three years?"

He closed his eyes. Chris was right. Maybe this was all his father's doing after all.

A few minutes later, Leo hung up and realized he was standing next to a pub. He read the sign. Tapas and Drinks.

Works for me.

He entered the dark room. When his eyes adjusted, he walked up to the bartender and ordered garlic fries and a beer. He grabbed his mug and sat in a booth.

He took a long drag on his drink, then decided it was time to move on and do what he was good at. Create things that people didn't realize they needed. And make a crap load of money doing it.

Time to move on. Leave this town and leave behind the people and memories.

"Hello, Mr. Moncrieff," a familiar voice said.

He looked up. Adela. He grinned. "This is not the type of place I would've expected you to frequent."

She nearly smiled. "I do not. But I was across the street and couldn't help but see you on an animated call. And then you walked into the tavern."

"You are very observant."

"I have to be," she said, then sat. "I make it my job to be aware of what happens in the town that for decades the Roca family has invested and reinvested in."

"Can I get you a drink?" he asked, but just then, a glass of white wine showed up in front of her.

"To your health," she said and took a sip.

He reciprocated and took another long pull.

"I'm going to take a guess," he said.

She urged him to continue.

"You know what happened this morning. And you have an opinion. Which is why you came here."

She smiled full-on, showing off her perfect teeth. "I do not know details. But I know how to make an educated guess."

She took another sip.

"The first time we met, I gave you some advice about Miss Alonzo."

"I remember," he said. His voice had hardened. Did he really want to hear this?

"Have you looked into her past? I mean, post your departure from Fortuny Bay?"

He studied her. "She has shared some details."

She took another sip. Her glass was empty now. "You may want to do some independent research."

She rose.

He got to his feet too. "What are you getting at?"

"History always has multiple views. You may discover that there is a version that does not align with her version."

"Maybe, but I know Catalina. I'm also a fairly good judge of character. And I sense nothing but decency in her."

She remained stoic for a few moments. "I will leave you with this. Are you certain you can be objective when it comes to her? I ask because I can tell you that when it comes to my children and grandchildren, I have a blind spot. I accept that and gladly accept all that comes with that."

He nodded. "And you think I may have a blind spot with her?"

She stepped back. "Only you can answer that. But you have to detach yourself and objectively view the situation." She glanced at her diamond-studded watch. "I should leave. As it is, I've said too much. I'm afraid alcohol has a tendency to loosen my lips."

Not for one second, did he believe that she was not completely in control of her faculties.

She reached the door, faced him, and said, "Be well, Leo."

After she was gone, he dropped back into his seat. No. That woman was intentional in everything she did. She knew exactly what she was saying.

She had shaken the hornet's nest. He needed to dig deeper. And he knew just the person who could dig on his behalf. Was there more to Cat that he wasn't seeing? And what was really wrong with his father? He pulled up the contact information of the private detective and called him.

[illegible] [illegible] [illegible] [illegible]
[illegible] [illegible] [illegible]
[illegible] [illegible] [illegible] [illegible]
[illegible] [illegible] [illegible]
[illegible] [illegible] [illegible] [illegible]
[illegible] [illegible] [illegible] [illegible]
[illegible] [illegible] [illegible] [illegible]
[illegible] [illegible] [illegible] [illegible]

[illegible] [illegible] [illegible] [illegible]
[illegible] [illegible] [illegible]
[illegible] [illegible] [illegible] [illegible]
[illegible] [illegible] [illegible]

[illegible] [illegible] [illegible] [illegible]
[illegible] [illegible] [illegible]
[illegible] [illegible] [illegible] [illegible]

[illegible] [illegible] [illegible] [illegible]
[illegible] [illegible] [illegible]

Chapter Thirty-One

Catalina

"That is amazing!" Lola said, her voice so loud that the phone distorted in Cat's ears.

That was not what she wanted to hear from her friend. "Okay, yes, it's amazing and generous and completely unexpected, but what about Leo?"

"This is exactly the type of break you needed. Think about what this means for you and Chicho. Finally, you will have financial security."

Lola was missing the point. "This was Leo's family home. For well over a hundred years. And now it's gone. Think of what he must be thinking of his dad now. Think of what he must be thinking of me."

Lola scoffed. "There's nothing to pin on you. You were not behind this. You didn't know anything about this. And frankly, you need this. He does not."

After trying to explain why Cat felt so bad for him a few more minutes, Cat gave up. Lola just wasn't getting it.

Cat tried calling him and texting him. Nothing. Cat paced in front of the kitchen window, facing his truck. Every perceived movement outdoors stopped her in her tracks. But so far, hours after she left Roberto's office, there was still no sign of Leo. His truck was still here, which meant he would show up at some point.

Unless a helicopter picked him up.

She shook her head, still unable to truly understand how much money he had.

She could understand feeling overlooked or slighted by his own dad. But she didn't want him to think that she had betrayed him.

She scanned the house. Her house. Truth be told, she didn't want this. She wanted to be in control of her life. Get her son and leave. Start fresh. If she could have a bit of savings to get themselves off the ground, then she'd be grateful. More than that would be a headache.

Movement caught her eye. She spun to the window and saw him. Phone pressed to his ear, he marched toward his car.

Crap! He's going to leave.

She ran outside to stop him.

When he saw her, he hesitated. Said something into the receiver, then lowered it.

"Give me a few minutes," he said. "I'll come and say goodbye before I leave."

She released the air she'd been holding. "Okay. Good. Please, do come in."

He nodded, then put the phone back to his ear and climbed into his car.

Well, at least he didn't yell at her, or throw something at her. That had to be a good sign. She walked back to the house and wondered what he was doing in the car. The windows were heavily tinted, but a rectangular source of light shone for a second.

Laptop?

He must've been working. That was also good news, she assumed. He was losing himself in the work. And he said he'd come in to say bye. He wasn't just cutting her off.

She paced inside, then scanned the kitchen.

She stared at the new refrigerator. The one he bought when he thought this was his house.

The threat of tears stung her eyes.

What was going on with her life? She didn't know how to manage all this. But she was certain that the people in town who wanted nothing but the worst for her would not be happy about her newfound financial independence.

A chill shook her to the bones.

Cat practically jumped when the kitchen door opened. She collected herself and marched from the study into the kitchen. He was washing his hands.

"Hey," she said.

He glanced at her over his shoulder. "Well, Cat. As much fun as this has been, it's time to call it a day. I'm leaving."

"Wait, not like this."

He dried his hands, then turned to face her. He leaned back against the sink. "Then how would you like me to leave?"

"Can we please sit and talk about what happened?"

He crossed his arms. "It's not too complicated, Cat. I can sum it up in one phrase."

She blinked.

"My dear father wanted to have the last laugh from the grave. What's hilarious is that he's not even buried, and he's laughing at me."

"No, that's not what happened," Cat said.

He put up his hands. "I don't hold any of this against you. And I get where you're coming from. He took care of you and Francisco. So it's natural that you'd come to his defense."

"I was defending him before I knew anything about this," she said. Now she was getting upset.

He scoffed.

"What is that? What does that mean?" She stepped toward him.

"He made sure that you'd get your 'and she lived happily ever after' moment."

"My happily ever after? You have no idea what I'm dealing with. Nothing in my life is pointing to the Hallmark Channel."

"You're right. I don't know what you're dealing with. And whose fault is that? You keep being elusive and speak in mysterious terms. If you want empathy, then you need to share. And let's be honest, this place is a bit of treasure. The second you list this house, you'll get a lineup of suitors."

She moderated her breathing. He had not listened to the will's instructions.

"Leo, you did me wrong ten years ago. The least, the bare minimum, you can give me is a conversation where you will listen and not jump to conclusions."

He blinked. His shoulders dropped a bit.

"Coffee and conversation. That's what I'm asking for."

He took a deep breath and nodded. "Sure. Why not?"

She poured the hot water over the instant coffee powder and put two mugs on the kitchen table, then sat. He joined her.

"I'm going to read you what was in the will. The part you missed."

"Is that necessary?" he asked.

"It is."

He wrapped his hands around the steaming mug and stared deeply into her eyes.

She unfolded the copy and read the relevant parts.

> The dream was for the house to be converted into a bed-and-breakfast. Catalina heard my non-stop visions for Casa Moncrieff over the years she took care of me. By now, the vision should be burnt into her mind.
>
> I do not want this home sold. I want it to stay with the family. I can't control what will happen once I'm gone. I realize that. I can just ask and hope this will be carried out according to my wishes.
>
> If the house remains a home for Catalina and

Francisco, I request that Lionel Jr.'s room be kept as-is.

If the house becomes a bed-and-breakfast, then I request that his room will always be available to him should he want to visit Fortuny Bay.

I also ask that my passion project be handed to Lionel Jr. as he may be the only one who can understand it.

Lastly, Catalina, I hope that this will give you a chance to finally win.

She folded the letter, then looked up at Leo.

His eyes were bloodshot. "What is this?" he said. His voice had an edge.

"What do you mean?"

"Is he playing with me? Why does he want you to always have my room available for me? What is this crap? Is this some sort of joke? Is he just trying to mess with me?"

She reached out and grabbed his hand. "No, Leo. There's one more letter. It was not read because you left. It was for you."

"You have it?" he asked.

She nodded and pulled the letter from her purse. She handed it to him, but he didn't take it.

"You read it," he said.

"He may have said something that's private... just for you."

"You read it," he said again.

She unsealed the envelope and unfolded the letter. She glanced at him, then back to the letter and read it out loud.

Son,

You've achieved a lot. Your mom always said you

would. She felt this town would hold you back. She was right. The house is now Catalina's. This is what I want. You don't need this place. You don't need more things. You need home, but I know this place never felt like much of a home to you. I have asked Catalina to always have a place for you should you ever want to return. I also hope that you will be a friend to her. She needs one.

Dad

The chair legs scraped the floor as Leo rose. He went to the fridge and pulled a couple of beers.

"You want?"

She shook her head.

He opened both, drained the first in seconds, then walked outside with the other bottle in hand.

She followed him outside. "Leo, talk to me."

He ran his hand through his hair, then spun. "Sure. What do you want me to talk to you about? What should I say? What should I feel? He's right. I don't need this house. I can buy anything I want. But I can't have everything I want."

His eyes bore into hers for a moment before he snapped away and took three long gulps, nearly draining the bottle.

"I wanted a regular family. Partially dysfunctional but intact. That's normal in my book. Nothing is perfect. Nothing. So, I'm really confused. My father called me names when I lived here. And now, he writes a letter that will not win any awards for love letters, but it sounds like a letter from a normal person. He was *not* normal."

Cat reached, took his bottle, and drank the rest of the beer. She then sat on the porch steps. He sat next to her.

"No, he was not," Cat said. "I remember those days. He was tough on you. I don't know why. But I know that not having you here was hard on him. There's no way he would keep your room like a museum showpiece otherwise. He was a proud man. Someone who didn't know how to show his feelings."

He laughed. "Feelings? He once said that men are meant to be strong. Self-control, he would growl when I'd get riled up over a baseball game or when my team lost. Self-control, Leo." He imitated his father's raspy voice. "Yeah, not Mr. Touchy Feely." He picked up the empty beer bottle, studied it, then forced a few drops in his throat.

"That's excellent beer," she said.

"Only the best will do." He sighed. "I could use another."

"I got it," she said. "Don't go anywhere."

"Yeah... fine."

She returned with two bottles. Handed one to him, then they toasted each other and drank some more.

"Glad you're drinking one, too."

"Nobody should drink alone when drinkin' is what's called for," she said. "Haven't had a beer for a good three years. Forgot that I used to like it."

Silence.

"I should leave," he said, more to himself as if engaged in a debate. Then he took another sip.

"No, you shouldn't. Stay here."

He glanced at her. "Are you drunk?"

"Not that drunk."

He laughed.

Chapter Thirty-Two

Leo

Leo's feet were on the porch railings. Chicho was fast asleep in Cat's embrace. Empty beer bottles and pizza boxes littered the back porch. The moon, though not full, somehow perfectly illuminated the ocean. No sea mist tonight. One of those rare nights where visibility was perfect.

He rose with difficulty. The world wobbled a bit with his movement. He may have overdone it with the drinks.

"This was your plan all along," he said. "Get me so sloshed that I couldn't drive back."

"You took on the task of sloshing all on your own," she said.

"Now, you'll try to take advantage of me." He sauntered close to her. He reached his hand toward her. Her eyes widened until she realized he was combing Chicho's matted hair.

"He's a good kid," Leo said.

"He's amazing."

"And you're a pretty good mom, Cat. The way you used to take care of plants, I was worried about this kid's chances."

"How dare you?"

He shrugged. "I'm rich. I can dare a lot of things and get away with it."

"Not around here."

He leaned against the railing to regain his balance. "You have no idea, Cat. The doors that open when you become part of that sphere."

"No, I can barely appreciate what it's like to have a guaranteed meal in the fridge every night."

He shifted to face her. "What's your plan? You gonna sell?"

She hesitated. "He was pretty clear in his—"

"Yeah, but even he acknowledged he can't stop you. I think you're ready to dump this place and run."

She took a deep breath. "Truth? I would love to separate myself from this town and be gone. But each time he talked about bringing *Casa Moncrieff* back to its original beauty, it would excite me. I admit, at times, I pictured myself preparing the food for the guests. It would be a dream come true to turn this place into a bed-and-breakfast. But this town... I don't know if I'll ever make it here."

"Because of what happened with Raf?"

She nodded. "I'm a leper here. They would love nothing more than to see me gone."

"A bit extreme, me-thinks. I mean, it's been over three years. Are you sure you're not reading into this whole thing? I mean, it's not like you're a black widow."

She remained silent.

"You're kidding," he said. "They think you're responsible for his death?"

"His family is very influential. All it takes is a well-placed rumor. Repeat it enough times and it becomes true. So when I was left with nothing, for some I got what I deserved."

He ran his hand over his stubbles. "So when my father took you in he must've gotten lip from the others."

Chicho adjusted himself in her arms.

"Of course. But you know him. He happily went to war with

anyone who wanted to go there. He lost friends and clients, including the entire harbor operations. But he no longer really wanted to work. He did their taxes out of a sense of obligation and because it's just what he did. It's what he was good at—tracking numbers and making sense of details. But if they were going to cut him off, he gladly cut right back. I hated that he lost business because of me."

Leo so wanted to find evidence that she was not on the up and up. He wanted to prove that she stole this house. He wanted to take ownership of his mom's house. But there was nothing. She was honest, decent, and genuinely confused. Chris had been right. Adela, not so much.

Chicho sat up. "I'm tired," he whispered.

"Let's go to bed," she said, and somehow, with athletic grace, she rose to her feet with Chicho tightly wrapped in her arms.

Leo eventually straightened on his own strength, then followed her upstairs to their bedroom. Two strategically placed twin beds took up most of the room. When she reached his bed, Leo quickly pulled the sheets open. She slid the little guy in and then covered him.

They stepped out.

"Thanks."

"M'pleasure."

They stood there in silence.

"Get your bags so I can lock the doors and windows," she said.

"I can sleep in the truck."

"Please, stay indoors," she said.

He studied her eyes. Something was wrong. "Is there something I should know?"

She took a step backward. "What do you mean?"

"The way you lock the doors and windows—"

"Nothing wrong with that," she jumped in.

"And then double-check each one...."

"I'm just thorough." She broke eye contact.

"Are you scared of something? Or someone?"

She blinked, then shook her head. "Just remnants of the past."

"The past?"

She put up a hand. "Go on. Get your stuff."

He didn't argue. He wasn't all there. All those beers had him less sharp than he'd like. But as he went to his truck, he scanned the surroundings. Nothing out of the ordinary. Was her fear really from the past, like some sort of PTSD thing? Or was there something she was fearing right now? Or were some in town out to get her?

But why would anyone really care about Raf? Okay, so his family had money. Probably. Did he become some sort of savior or hero to these people here? They must've been part of the commercial fishing economy, which would explain the boating accident. What type of work did they do that set him apart from her? It's not like Fortuny Bay generated the type of business that Morro Bay or Avila produced. Something didn't add up.

He grabbed his bags and locked up the car. He took another cursory look, but again, nothing.

Cat was already at the door, waiting for him to come in. "Got everything?"

"Yeah."

She locked the door after he slid in. She then cracked the curtain open, looked outside for good measure, then turned off the back porch light.

"Give me your soiled clothes. I can put them in the washer overnight."

Leo followed her to the machine. He couldn't recall the last time he'd done his own laundry. He used to do it all the time. Even after he left college and after he sold his first company. Somehow, in a moment lost to time, he stopped. His house crew took over cleaning duties. Things were always done. Like magic. Whether he left the clothes on the floor, in the yard, or in the hamper — the next day, they were clean and ready for use.

Funny how basic things that had been part of his life for so many years disappeared, and he hadn't even realized they were gone. What else had he forgotten since he got so busy and so wealthy that those details were outsourced — someone else's problem?

"Give me that," he told her. "You don't have to do my laundry."

She froze, then moved out of the way. "Is it because you don't want me to see your underwear?"

"Something like that." He studied the antique. He had used this machine when he lived here. It was like riding a bike. Or so he assumed. He stumbled for a few seconds, then it came back to him.

"Well done," she said. "I guess the training your mom gave you stuck. This will take a while, though. Let's get you settled in your room."

They quietly walked up the stairs together.

"I think you know where everything is," she said.

"Yeah, I do." A beat. "You kept my ring."

She slowed down, then glanced at him. "What?"

"I saw it on your key chain."

"Oh that," she said nonchalantly. She ran her hand through her hair. "Yeah, slid it on many years ago, and now it's just part of the bling. You know... looks nice."

He nodded. "Thank you," he said as they reached the second floor landing.

She turned and faced him. "For what?"

"For not getting rid of it."

She shrugged and studied the floor. "Wel... I thought about it. Many times. But no matter how much I wanted to... I just couldn't." She hesitated. "I don't know why I'm telling you all this. Must be the wine and beers."

He touched her chin and gently redirected her eyes toward him. Cat's eyes widened, but she did not blink. She held his gaze.

Her scent, her body, her eyes—her presence—caused him to lose all self-control.

He thought of things he could say. But words were not what was needed. He didn't want a conversation or a discussion. He wanted her.

He brought her lips to his. The familiar, the perfect, the once-forgotten shook him to his core. He tasted her mouth for the first time in over a decade.

Over the years, he had thought about her many times. He had seen her face on the faces of strangers, pretending, imagining that it was her. But all those moments and all his memories did not match the reality he was experiencing right now.

Their lips lingered, tasted, and remembered why they had been so good for each other. But now, she was more tender, more loving, and more wonderful than anything he could've hoped for. Their mouths melted together—muscle memory? No, just perfection—like music, like waves on the shore—built for each other.

His heart continued to hammer against his chest. Suddenly, he was out of breath and lightheaded.

Her hands landed on his chest. She gently created distance, separating their lips. He opened his eyes. Hers were already open and red-rimmed.

"Leo?" she stammered.

Her face began to blur.

What's going on?

He reached backward and steadied himself on the stair railings, then closed his eyes so that the whirling world would stop. "What the —" he got out, just as his right knee wobbled.

"Hey," she said, then quickly grabbed him.

Sweat broke out at the nape of his neck. He took a deep breath.

"What's going on?" she asked.

He took another lung full of air. Her scent gave him the much needed burst of temporary clarity. "I'm okay. I think... just need to get to bed."

He grabbed the rails and pulled himself up toward the third floor.

"Let me help you," Cat said as she grabbed his side and walked him up.

Her touch was dangerous. "I'm good," he said. "I got this." He stepped out of her hold and willed himself up the stairs. As he made the turn, he chanced a glance at her. She stood frozen, tracking him. Or was that shock on her face?

Oh man. What have I done?

Chapter Thirty-Three

Leo

Leo blinked his tired eyes open and smiled. Through the threadbare curtains the sun broke in. The glare of the sun took him back to all those years ago. He could never really sleep in during those summer mornings. Almost like the sun was in on the conspiracy to make sure that every summer day started early.

His neck felt tight. And a heaviness draped over his head. He forced himself up. The bed complained. That had to be the most uncomfortable mattress ever. Even so, he had slept deeply. The smell of the laundry detergent on these sheets was like home. Well, it was. His father was a creature of habit. Why change something that worked fine, he would've said.

Of course, Leo was also a good thirty pounds of muscle heavier. He used to be scrawny, at best. When he finally met Chris face to face in college, he became motivated by Chris's addiction to leverage exercise to keep his energy levels high. Workout. Shower. Nap. Then up for another eight hours of uninterrupted work.

Maybe that's what he needed to break this... whatever this was that had him all tight and off.

Hangover.

That's what it was. He had been drinking all day yesterday. He hesitated. A thought tried to break through, but didn't.

He got out of bed and stretched. That was more difficult than he expected. He had not exercised for a good minute. Not that he could. There was no gym here.

Old school, he decided.

He dropped to the floor and hammered away at pushups. Wide, narrow, diamond. The blood flow was exactly what he needed. Next, he executed squats, lunges, and then finally a battery of ab and core exercises.

He put in a good ten minutes. Not great, but good enough in this environment. He grabbed his toiletries and strode to the bathroom that was across from his room. He flipped the lights on and found a clean towel on the counter. Cat was always a step ahead. He grinned, but then immediately frowned.

In that instant, he remembered everything that had happened just as the night came to an end. He covered his face with his hands.

Crap, crap, crap!

So typical of him to just avoid the memories and implications. He'd gotten so good at that. What had he been thinking?

How would he clean this up? He forced himself to remember her face as he walked upstairs. She was mad. She was hurt.

Stupid, stupid!

He turned the shower handle, and while he waited for the water to warm up, he brushed his teeth. He needed to think. He was confused, no doubt about it. But it was unfair to dump his confusion into her lap. He didn't even know if she was over the passing of Raf. She was still secretive, but that could be understandable. He was by far the last person she'd trust with something that was hard to relive.

Did she still love Raf, he wondered?

Leo gargled, then took out the razor kit. He looked at the growth on his face. He preferred the razor-sharp clean look. Somehow, this thing that had taken shape on his face over the past few days didn't look horrible. Unkempt, but then again, that is how he felt—rundown.

What were his options with Cat? He could just come out and apologize. One more apology to add to the list? No. There had to be another option.

He checked the water. Lukewarm, like always. He marched in and soldiered through. He had gotten so used to hot, super hot water that this seemed like some sort of torture or Navy Seals training.

He stared at the shower-head that practically spat at him. He visualized his home shower. It was an embarrassment of fortunes. He scanned the dark, damp tub-slash-shower. When he hadn't known any better, this was as good as things got. After all, he had his own bathroom. It was surprising that all in all, this place had withstood the unrelenting attacks of time.

And here he was, indirectly attacking Cat during a time she needed a friend. He knew her well enough to know that she would not put up with this behavior.

He shut off the water, grabbed the towel, and, after drying most of his body, he wrapped the towel around his hips. He cracked the door open to make sure she hadn't come upstairs. No sign of the lady of the house.

Her house. Not his. It was still hard for him to digest that the house was no longer in his family.

He strolled toward his room.

"Breakfast?" she called out from downstairs.

He hesitated. "Sounds great."

"Okay," she said.

For a moment, he wanted to convince himself that the kiss had never happened. Or maybe she didn't remember either. She had been drinking also.

That was his solution. Pretend that he was so plastered that he could barely remember details. One thing was for sure. He needed to leave. Staying here was not good for his health. This place and Cat were persistent reminders that he was really an outsider. Also, the more time he spent with her, the more he remembered the old days and the more he risked falling for her. He needed to leave the past in the past. He entered his room and locked the door.

Why was he even here? She'd asked him to stay, not because she missed his company or wanted to be with him. He'd drunk more than he should've. But his truck's automatic navigation system could've taken him home.

So why did he stay?

What had he hoped for?

As he shook his head, he noticed the clean clothes on his bed. Even his bed was made.

She didn't have to do that. In fact, she shouldn't do that. She was not his servant. After all, he was a guest in her home. But at the same time, if she was really mad at him, wouldn't she have thrown all his stuff out on the dirt? What if she was falling for him?

No!

He couldn't do that to her. He couldn't be selfish and take her down that path.

He took a long look through what used to be his room. It was time to cut the cord.

Leo changed, put all his belongings into his luggage, and headed downstairs.

He'd face the music, then head back home. His actual home. This was no longer his place.

Leo entered the kitchen to the now-familiar buttery smell of scrambled eggs. He released his luggage, which rolled smoothly toward the wall. Cat was staring out of the kitchen window toward the horizon, her hands on the counter.

"Smells good," he said.

She spun and quickly wiped at her eyes. "Hey," she said, sniffed, then collected herself. "Didn't hear your footsteps."

He studied her. Her nose was red, her cheeks flushed.

This was his fault. He had done this to her. Don't ask. Don't ask.

"What's wrong?" he asked.

"Nothing, nothing." When her eyes landed on his luggage, she froze. "Are you leaving?" she asked, her voice low.

"Yeah. It's time. We both know it."

She steadied herself on the headrest of a chair. And suddenly a tear drop skidded down her cheek.

He quickly stepped up to her and lifted her chin, bringing her eyes to meet his. "What's going on, Cat?"

She blinked. "I'm scared."

"Of what?"

She shook her head. "Of being on my own. Of being out of my depth. I can't do this."

What was she saying? Did she want him to stay with her? He helped her down to the chair and planted himself next to her. He held her hands in his.

"What is it you need to do that you don't think you can?"

She wiped at a tear. "The bed-and-breakfast. The clean-up. The planning. Where do I even start? Do I get a general contractor—whatever that is? Do I even have enough to pay for the work? I don't even know how to get cash to pay for the bills that have come. He had passwords to sites. He showed me once, but now, I can't recall what was for what. How am I supposed to—?"

This wasn't about them. He was safe. This was about this house. This he could help with. "Slow down, okay? One step at a time. You're overwhelming yourself. Do what's important first. Then the next and then the next."

She wiped her face once again. "But it's all important."

"Well, from where I'm sitting, the most important thing right now is the most obvious."

She leaned in. "Which is?"

"Eggs. We have to eat first. Nothing gets done on an empty stomach."

She studied his eyes. Another tear rolled down. This time, he wiped it with his thumb.

"Don't cry. You're not on your own. You have Lola. You have Roberto. You have... you know. Me."

"Do I have you? Or will I be a distant memory once you leave again? Will it be another ten years from now when you remember someone that you used to know?"

He offered a faint smile. "Yeah, you have me."

"I hope so," she said, her voice barely audible.

"Now, can I have my eggs?"

They finished breakfast and placed their forks down on their plates at the same time. They held onto each other's gaze for a few moments.

"I really want to hate you," she said.

"I know."

"And I don't want to forgive you."

He nodded. "I get that."

"But you make it really, really hard for me to stick to my guns."

He shrugged. "It's a gift."

She dropped her hand on his. "Is it? Or is it a curse?"

Leo's eyebrows rose. "A curse?"

"How were you able to walk away and never look back? Did you not think of us? Did it ever hurt? Are you able to so easily... what do they call it...?"

"Compartmentalize," he offered.

She snapped her fingers. "That's the one. Are you able to just compartmentalize and focus on what you have to and not let that other stuff affect you in any way?"

He pulled his hand out of her grasp and sat back. "We all deal with things in different ways. We find ways to silence that voice." He moved the fork on his plate. "We all have demons."

She studied him. "And how do you compartmentalize last night?"

He froze, then stammered. It was now or never. Time to man up. "Last night?" he asked. "You mean the drinking?"

Her eyes were gentle. "Yeah, the drinking," she said. "Maybe we shouldn't drink that much again."

She gave him a pass. "Okay," he said. But as he uttered the word, he could taste the wine on her lips all over again.

"Hi," Chicho said, his voice groggy.

They both straightened. "Good morning, sleepyhead," she said.

"Hey, buddy. How are you?"

"I'm good. Mommy, I'm hungry."

She switched into mom mode and started preparing Chicho's breakfast.

Chicho sat next to Leo. "Are we going to the beach?" Chicho asked.

"No, sweetie," Cat said. "Leo is going back to his home today."

"Okay," Chicho said. "What should I take with me, Mommy?"

They both stared at him. "Take where?" she asked.

"To Leo's house. Remember what you said last time?"

She smiled. "Maybe another time."

Chicho's face straightened. "When you say that, it means we won't do it."

"That's not true," she said.

Chicho turned to Leo. "Do you promise?"

"Yeah, definitely. I promise."

Leo felt Cat's eyes on him. Leo glanced at her. Her eyes were hard and tortured at the same time. He had promised her also, many years ago. But this was different. She had to know that.

"Good news is that I'm not leaving right now," Leo added. "I've got to help your mom with some stuff around the house."

"I can help, too," Chicho said.

"I'm counting on you."

"I can do it," Chicho said with determination.

Leo put out his fist. Chicho bumped it.

"Done deal," Leo said.

"Done deal."

Chapter Thirty-Four

Catalina

Cat watched Leo do his thing in awe. He was clear-minded. Focused. Determined. He certainly knew how to make a cup of coffee.

Apparently, he had ordered a bunch of things when he thought this would be his place. Amazon Delivery dropped off dozens of packages right after they finished breakfast.

He looked like a kid opening gifts.

"Here you go," he said as he handed Cat a cup of coffee that looked like the ones she used to drink when she was married. Back when money covered the sadness and fear.

She took a sip and smiled.

"Dang, that's a good cup of jo," she said.

"Me too, Ma!" Chicho said.

"No, no, it's not good for you," she said.

"Then why is it good for you?"

He had a good point. "What if I give you a spoonful?"

He didn't respond. Instead, he ran to the cutlery drawer and pulled out a soup spoon.

She scooped off a bit, blew on it, hoping it had cooled sufficiently. "Here. Drink it like you drink hot soup."

"Making that sound?"

Leo laughed. They both looked at him. "Don't mind me. I'm just happy I can drink real coffee."

Chicho hesitantly approached the spoon and slurped. His mouth contorted, and he shook his face.

"Agh," he yelled. "It's not good."

Cat smiled. Mission accomplished. The kid would not ask for coffee for a good five years.

Leo took a sip of his. "Ahh, here's to not good coffee."

Chicho stared at him in shock, then turned to Cat. "Can I have hot chocolate?"

"I can do that with this machine!" Leo said.

Chicho looked at Cat, fear in his eyes. "Will that taste good?"

She pulled him into an embrace and laughed like she hadn't laughed in years. Maybe an entire decade.

Cat and Leo marched into Lionel senior's study and scanned the room. Where to start? Her heart rate picked up again. Her shoulders slumped. This was all on her now.

"First thing we're gonna do," he said, "is not panic."

She faced him. He could still read her. Although in those early days, she was not the panicking type. She had no reason to worry about anything.

"Okay," she said.

He placed his laptop on his dad's desk. "Let's see," he said as he scanned the room for something specific. "That'll do." He pointed to the closet door mirror.

The study, which was actually a converted bedroom, had double mirrored closet doors. He opened his leather backpack. From it, he pulled out dry erase markers.

"You travel with markers?" she asked.

"It's a staple product. I need to write things when working with the teams." He took the red marker and handed it to Chicho. "Come with me," he said. He drew a line on the mirror separating the top and bottom. "We need you to inspire us with drawings. The bottom half is yours. The top is ours."

Chicho looked at his mom. "Can I draw?"

She took the marker from Leo's hand and drew a line. "This one can be erased," she said, and proved it by running her thumb over it. "But only on the mirror. Don't start drawing on walls."

His eyes lit up. "Awesome!" he said, then started experimenting.

"Okay," Leo said. "We're going to make a list."

"Of what?"

"Of everything you can think of that needs to be done."

"Oh, my..." she sighed.

"But we're splitting the list in three. On the left side will be things that need to be done in the next ten days. The middle column will be for those that need to be done in the next ninety days. The right side is long-term plans."

"Like the bed-and-breakfast?"

"Exactly. They're important but not urgent. In other words, we don't want to forget, but we don't have to act on them now."

She appreciated this. And she felt a sense of relief that he said 'we.'

"Okay," she said. Hope softened her voice.

"Here's the deal: don't worry about what they imply. Some are big. Some are small. Those that are big, we will convert into smaller tasks. We want to get things crossed off the list. We want to see completion. We want to see closure."

"Got it."

She started. She wrote everything she'd been stressing over. Things that had not allowed her to sleep. She even put down things that were questions.

"Hey Cat?" he called out.

She turned to him. "Sup?"

He was in his father's chair, leaning back, arms crossed. "What did he mean when he wrote about his passion project? What is that?"

She closed the cap of the marker and strolled up to the desk. "I honestly don't know." She sat on the ledge. "Before he got very ill, he'd spend hours researching things on the internet. Twice I heard him on the phone asking for historical information. He'd call libraries to get details from decades ago."

"But you didn't know what he was searching for?"

She shook her head.

He tapped on the journal that they'd flipped through a couple of days ago. "Do you think this has anything to do with it?"

She shrugged. "He was very secretive when it came to some things. When he used to go out on late-night strolls, he never wanted me to join him. So I'd watch him from the porch. If I walked into his office when he was working, he'd change the screen."

Leo's eyes bore into her. "What was he up to? And how am I supposed to work on it if he didn't leave me more details?"

"Maybe you can find it in here somewhere." She waved her hands, gesturing the entire office.

"He sure was a packrat," Leo said.

"That he was. He would not allow me to throw anything out."

"You'll need to add a task called 'organize' because the entire house needs to go through that."

"Yeah... that's a monster." She returned to the mirror and added that task. As she wrote, she heard what sounded like a phone call, but it was coming from his computer.

"Mornin' Anna," he said.

Cat turned to his voice and on the screen she saw the woman he'd spoken to a couple of days earlier.

"Where are you?" she asked.

"Fortuny Bay. Are you busy today?"

"I work for you. So yes, I'm busy."

He rolled his eyes. "Anything urgent?"

"No."

"Can you come here for a day or two?"

Cat stopped writing and faced him.

"Why?" Anna asked.

"I have a fun project for you."

"Ugh. Do I need to update my resume?"

He scoffed. "Seriously. You'll love this. Remember how you went all military a few months back with organizing, minimizing... all that crap?"

"It is *not* crap!"

He held his hand out in surrender. "Fine. Not crap. This house could use a expert. But I want someone that a) I can trust, and b) will look for the details that most eyes don't see." He hesitated. "Intrigued?"

"You had me at 'organize.'"

"Get our facilities guys to identify a couple of strong kids to come here so they can move boxes, books, etc. But also a couple of analysts. People that can flip through detailed files and books and capture data."

"Got it," she said. "But I need to get some... stuff."

"Stuff?"

"Yeah. Tools. Equipment."

"Sure. Get what you need." He turned to Cat. "Sorry, Cat. I'm in total command-and-control mode. I should've asked you first. Are you okay with getting help?"

She smiled so wide her face hurt. "I would love the help." And she couldn't deny that the thought of having more people here gave her a sense of comfort and safety.

"Cool!" he said and returned to Anna. "Can you be here today? You'll need a couple of days of clothing and—"

"Sure," Anna said. "I can be there in maybe four hours. I need to get labels, and markers, and boxes, and—"

He tapped the screen, then turned to Cat. "I've created a monster. But we need expert help."

"I really appreciate this."

"You still want to hate me?"

"Big time."

[illegible]

Leo

Sitting side-by-side behind the desk, Leo and Cat methodically went through every utility bill and found that his father had already set up automatic payments. They moved on to the bank accounts. The call with the bank proved that the paperwork that should've been processed by Roberto was not completed yet. Months ago, his father had already put her on his accounts. She hadn't realized that the notarized document she signed was actually giving her authority over Lionel senior's bank accounts. She thought it was so that she could sign checks for him. With that already in place, transferring the funds into her account should've been easy. But Roberto had to turn in some more documents to the bank.

"Dial him and pass me the phone," he said.

"Why don't you call him?"

He stared at her. "What? And let him have my number? Very few get my number."

"What? No phone number spoofing capability on your device.

Even Raf had it on his. I thought you were a technologist." She dialed the phone and handed it to him.

Why would Raf need spoofing capability on his phone?

"Hi Catalina, how can I help you?" Roberto said.

"Hey, it's Leo. The bank says they can't transfer my father's money because they have not received the proper paperwork yet."

A pause. "That's odd. I sent a scanned file yesterday."

"Shoot it over to Cat's email. We'll take care of it," he said.

"Let me follow up. I'm sure it's just a mix-up."

Leo didn't like delays. "Do that after you email the scanned file. It should be in your sent folder. Just forward it from there. I'll wait while you do it."

Cat pushed his shoulder. He turned to her and mouthed, 'what?'

"Be nice," she whispered.

He frowned. If he didn't push, she'd be waiting for weeks.

"Sure," Roberto said. Some thirty seconds later, he said, "I just sent it."

"One sec," Leo said, then turned to Cat. "Did you get it?"

She refreshed her phone. "Got it," she said.

"Thank you, Mr. Chaparral," he said and hung up. "While he's calling them, we'll just do a couple of things here."

He opened a bank account for her with the same bank. This would make the process easier.

"Can we do that?" she asked, leaning forward, inches away from him.

Man, she smelled nice.

Stop that.

He focused on the task at hand. "We can," he said after getting his head back on the task at hand. "And we just did. Hopefully, Roberto will take care of the issue. We can then merge the accounts and get you an ATM card."

"I can't thank you enough, Leo. This is such a weight lifted off me." She leaned back in her chair.

"Once the money is fully under your name, you'll want to go back to the utility accounts and do a transfer under your name. You'll build credit this way." He looked at his watch. "Where's Anna?"

And just as he spoke her name, his phone rang. Her name and picture filled the screen. Of course she called when he thought of her. They were always on the same wavelength.

"What happened to you?" he asked.

"Almost there. What should've taken 15 minutes took an hour. Service is dead, I tell you."

"True," he said.

"The satellite photo of the property shows that there's a fairly large lot to the side of the house. Is that accurate?"

"Yes," he said. "Why?"

"Well... I'm here. Ah, there's your monstrosity of a truck."

"Coming outside now," he said. And just then, a horn blared.

"What was that?" Cat asked.

He shrugged. "I'm almost afraid to go outside."

"Wow!" Chicho yelled. "That's awesome!"

They all went outside. As the plume of dust settled, a huge, forty-foot RV emerged.

"What has she done?" he breathed.

The side door opened, and out walked a beaming Anna. "Isn't she awesome?"

Leo walked up to her and exchanged high fives. "Did I buy this?" he asked.

"No, you're renting it." She hesitated. "You have hair growing on your face."

He frowned. "Thanks for noticing. Why do I need this?"

"I need it. It's my central command center. Yes, I know central and center are kinda the same thing but it sounds cool. All important files, including the family pictures, will come in here."

Cat joined them. "Can we check out the inside?" she asked. Chicho was peeking at the RV from behind his mom.

"You must be Catalina. Give us a hug," Anna said.

"She's a hugger," Leo said.

They embraced. Anna lowered herself to Chicho's eye level. "And who is this young man?"

"I'm Chicho."

"You wanna go inside?"

He nodded emphatically.

"Let's go," Anna said, and the three of them rushed inside. He loved how Anna took any situation by the reins and run with it. Suddenly, the RV expanded sideways.

He stepped inside the RV and froze. This thing was a tech masterpiece. A full mobile office. He walked past the others and went to the back, directly to the bedroom and master shower. It was huge.

"I'm staying here," he yelled out.

"Not gonna happen," Anna said. "This is my war room. Get your own."

"But I'm paying for it."

"And I'm very grateful for your generosity. Now, get out of my bedroom. It's not appropriate."

He scanned the work area. She had everything she needed to get the job done.

"Now, point me in the right direction. We have work to do."

Chapter Thirty-Six

Catalina

Cat's phone rang. Roberto once again.

"Hi, Roberto. Let me pass the—"

"No, no. I called to speak to you." A hesitation. "Can we speak privately?"

She paused, surprised, then moved toward the RV's door. "Sure. What's up?" She looked over her shoulder. Leo was tracking her movement.

"This is a sensitive topic, so I want you to please hear my heart in this. Because I care for you."

He did? That was interesting. He barely knew her. He only spoke to her on the last days of Lionel's life. And because Lionel had trusted him, that had been good enough for her. But to claim that he cared for her... well, that was unexpected.

"Thank you," she said, wondering where this was going. She exited the RV.

"I realize that you're probably feeling overwhelmed."

She laughed. "I am," she said, but the jungle ahead of her looked more and more manageable in the short half a day she had spent with Leo.

"Exactly," he said. "It's too much for anyone. I wish Lionel senior had told me. I could've been better prepared to help you during this transition."

That was an interesting point. Why had Lionel gone to the other fellow in San Luis Obispo? Why not him? He had actually even made that Maroutian guy the executor.

She elected to remain silent, encouraging him to speak on.

"But we are where we are. I worry…"

"What are you worried about?" she asked.

"I know Leo wants to help you. But there are two things that I can't shake. One, we all saw his reaction to the will reading. He did *not* seem to be supportive of this decision."

He was right about that.

"And two, even if his intention is truly to help you…."

He drifted. *Truly?* Was he implying that Leo wasn't really trying to help?

"The thing is that he may give you poor counsel. He may not be giving you the advice that is ideal for your specific situation."

Leo stepped out of the camper. They made eye contact. He put up a thumb, asking her if all was well. She returned the thumbs up and walked further away toward the front of the property.

"My situation," she repeated.

"Yes. With all that's going on and what will happen in the coming weeks and months. I suspect he's not aware of what's happening in your personal circumstance."

"He does not," she confirmed, and she wanted that fact to remain intact.

"Right," he said. "The real question is, what is the best course of action for you, both short term and long term?"

She sat on a boulder on the edge of the property.

"What do you recommend?"

She heard him take a deep breath. "Sell the property. Get the cash out and sit on it. You will then come from a strong financial position to... to... defend your situation."

"Sell it... and not do what Lionel asked me to do."

"Catalina, it is very noble that you'd want to fulfill a wish. But that is just a dream. Some things should remain a dream. It's an unfair burden to place on you. Life circumstances sometimes dictate a different, a more pragmatic, approach."

She rose from the boulder. She did not want to hear much more. "You're probably right. Thank you for this solid advice, Roberto," she said. "I am feeling so many emotions right now that I think I need to sleep on it and consider what's best for Francisco and me."

"Exactly. That's exactly what I'm recommending," he said.

"Thanks again—"

"One more thing," he said.

She reached the camper and paused.

"If I may be so bold. Please make sure that all the accounts that are being set up for you are being done correctly."

Her brows shut up. "Correctly?"

"Yes. I can't tell you how many people I've seen sign the wrong things, agree on questionable terms, and, in the end, give away everything that was rightfully theirs."

Was he saying Leo would try to rip her off? She almost laughed, but she controlled herself.

The reality of her situation—of her life so far—was that no one was trustworthy. Even Lionel senior's motivations had been suspect initially. But in the end, he always showed himself as the person she had hoped he'd be—a father figure who rose up when even her own parents disowned her.

"Thank you, Roberto. I'm going to go over everything carefully. Just to be on the safe side."

"Excellent. Thank you for trusting me. We will speak later," he said.

They hung up.

Trusting you? Yeah. She definitely felt something right now—trust was not exactly what she'd call it.

Chapter Thirty-Seven

Leo

The help arrived shortly after Anna. Two guys helped move boxes upon boxes of files. They also moved all the photos and negatives to the RV. Two analysts also showed up to flip through books and files. Anna was busy organizing those teams while Leo and Cat focused on the rest of the house. Lola also joined the party. She took Chicho with her to the park.

Leo noticed that ever since the phone call with Roberto, something was different with Cat. He asked, but she changed the topic. He would not dwell on what he couldn't control.

The good news was that the study was nearly done. It was time to take on the next challenge. "Let's go upstairs," he said, and she followed him up the creaky steps. There was a room that needed to be addressed, and today.

"Cat, we need to go through the master bedroom." He placed his hand on the handle of the closed door.

She froze. "No, I can't do that. Too soon."

"He gave this house to you, and you're sharing a room with Francisco."

She shook her head. "I haven't been able to go into his room since he…"

"I'm going in with you. At some point, it has to happen. It'll be easier to make decisions while I'm still here."

She leaned against the adjacent wall as she studied him. "This is weird."

"You're telling me. I'm helping my ex wash clean the memories of the house that used to be my home."

She dropped her head. "I… don't…."

"I'm not saying that to guilt you. It's a fact. I had to swallow it and move on. And so do you."

She faced him and held his gaze. "You're right."

"I'm leaving in a few hours. Let's get some more work done before I book."

Her eyes betrayed her. Was he completely misreading her? It seemed like she did not want him to leave. Was she feeling something for him again? She hadn't slapped him when he kissed her the night before. Or maybe it wasn't him, per se, but instead, she didn't want to be alone.

"Why don't you stay until the funeral?" she asked.

He shook his head. "I got to get on and go on. I'll be back for the funeral. But I think we both know that I am dangerously close to wearing out my welcome." He turned the handle.

"You're always welcome here. It will always be your other home."

He smiled. "Thanks, Cat. Now, let's see what we have to deal with."

She nodded, and with that, they stepped into the room he hadn't entered since the passing of his mom.

They sat on the bed and scanned the room. On paper, the bedroom would prove to be one of the easier rooms to address. But when it came to matters of the heart, this was a difficult one.

"We should give the clothes to the Salvation Army or something," Leo said.

"Your mom's clothes can help battered women's groups. They're always looking for donations."

He paused, then slowly turned to her and studied her profile. Why did she know that?

She faced him, ready to say something, but stopped when she realized he'd been looking at her. "What?" she asked, then tucked her hair behind her ear.

"Nothing," he said. "Was thinking that it's a great idea."

"Unless you want to keep her stuff... you know, as a memory or something."

"As a matter of fact..." he said, then rose off the bed and went to the closet and pulled the red jacket she used to wear when they went to parties. He also pulled down her flamenco dress and hat. She looked so amazing in those. He placed them on the bed, then turned to her dresser and opened her drawer, and got her scarfs.

He pulled them to his face and took a deep breath. He imagined that they still had her scent. He willed his mind to believe it.

"She told me she got these in Paris," he said. "Back then, it sounded like she was talking about a magical place." He added them to his loot. "The first time I went there, every store I passed on the Champs-Élysées, I imagined Mom and Dad window shopping, happy and in love."

"Wow," Cat said.

He turned to her. "What?"

"You just called your dad dad."

His brow rose. "A slip of the tongue." He grinned, then walked back to the closet and pulled down the zipper on an article of clothing. "That's the one," he said, then added it to the rest of the clothes.

She rose and opened the bag. "His military uniform? I didn't know he still had that."

"Let's find his cap," he said. They pulled a chair to look at the shelves in the closet.

"Here it is," she said, and she pulled down a box.

"I got one too," he said. They brought their boxes back to the room and sat on the floor to open them up.

Her's contained Lione Seniors hat. His contained something completely different.

Articles. Press clippings. Print outs. Story after story highlighting Leo's accomplishments. From his first company sale to the rumors of the acquisition of Vitruvian.

He placed all the clippings back in the box and closed the lid.

Cat draped her arm around his shoulder.

Her touch could still move him, to destabilize him. She was so close, so much like it used to be. She was exactly who he needed right now. No one else, not even Anna, could appreciate why these findings were completely messing with him.

"Are you okay, Leo?"

He chuckled. "I suppose. I just... I don't understand how he could've been so interested in my career and so intent on not letting my room be touched, but it was all done in secret. Why not speak to me? Why not call me, visit me, something, anything?"

"He didn't know how to be anything other than who he was. But clearly his heart was always on the right track."

"To think we could've had a different life, a different outcome."

She ruffled his hair. "Unknowable. Impossible to know what would've happened if things had been different between you two."

He eyed her. "What do you mean?"

"I think what drove you to be a mega-success was in some part because of the relationship you had with your dad."

"Or the relationship I didn't have."

"Same difference."

Her phone rang. She frowned when she saw Roberto's name on the screen. She breathed out, then answered it. "Hi Roberto," she said, her voice tight. Then her eyes softened. "Really? When?" Her eyes widened. "One sec." She covered the phone. "Leo, he says we can have the funeral tomorrow by early afternoon."

Leo flinched. "How? I thought—"

She shrugged. "Does it matter? Closure."

He nodded. "Let's do it."

She returned to the call, confirmed the time and place, then hung up. "That's that. I guess you're staying one more night."

He liked that she wanted him there. He wasn't sure why, but remaining close to her, to the house, and what secrets were hiding in her mind and in his father's study was definitely a good thing.

Chapter Thirty-Eight

Catalina

Cat and Leo went through all his parent's belongings and separated them into four piles: give away, keep, sell, and toss. Hardly anything entered the sell category. And the keep category was minimal, containing items that Leo wanted, or she'd want to keep. By the end, they filled multiple large bags with clothes. Two boxes stored the few items that would be kept. Another batch went into disposal boxes for those items that could not be given away.

Anna told them that a small trash trailer would arrive the next day, probably while they were at the small, private funeral. Tonight, they were expecting a courier who would deliver clothes for Leo. He didn't think attending a funeral in flip-flops would be right. Cat agreed.

She didn't know what Anna and the analysts had been up to, nor what had been found. That was not her business. What Leo had insisted on was to change the bedsheets and prepare the room to be ready for her to use for the first time.

As they finished changing the sheets, he excused himself and went

"

to the master bathroom. She was dusting the furniture when he came out.

"The room looks great."

She appraised it and smiled. "Yeah. I'm glad you forced me to do this."

"I just talked you into it."

"Call it what you will. It's done."

"Yup," he said. "Except for the bathroom. We never went through that stuff."

She sighed.

"I'll grab a box from downstairs and be right back."

She entered the bathroom and started with the medicine cabinet. She stopped when she opened it. Someone had arranged all the prescription bottles perfectly. *Leo?* Why would he align the bottles?

"Here we go," he said from behind her.

She brushed off the question and started emptying everything into the container.

The analysts and the muscle had already left. The other rooms that had been packed with old unstable furniture were now completely empty. In the process of cleaning up and organizing, the dream of getting closer to having a bed & breakfast became a little more realistic. *We now have vacant rooms*, she thought. And she hadn't even touched the other family rooms downstairs that'd been left covered and forgotten for years. But that was for another day.

Cat, Leo, Anna and Chicho were lounging on the back porch, watching the beautiful colors that the fading sun cast on the ocean. They devoured the food that Anna had picked up, and the wine was doing what wine does.

"This is amazing," Anna said.

"That it is," Leo said.

"Was it always this beautiful?" she asked.

"No," he said.

"Don't listen to him," Cat said. "He chose not to see the beauty of this place."

"Can I have ice cream?" Chicho asked.

"At this hour?" Cat asked and checked her phone's clock.

"It's not late, Mama."

She noticed a text from Roberto. *Now what?*

"Mama?"

"Yeah, okay, go for it."

Chicho ran off. Leo and Anna were discussing something, but she was focused on the text from Roberto.

> Someone from the clinic told me an investigator was asking questions about Lionel's death. He has power of attorney from Leo and is asking for all medical records. Why? Something doesn't feel right.

She looked up at Leo, who was now laughing.

He glanced at his watch. "Let's go to the scenic spot. I want to see something," he said. "Cat, you coming?"

She shook her head and forced a smile. "You two go on ahead. I'll hang out here with Chicho."

They did.

Why would he want to know about his dad's medical records? What was he looking for, she wondered? Then she recalled the medicine cabinet. Was he trying to find foul play?

She felt her face flush.

He wouldn't do that? Would he? Did he suspect her?

Anger rose in her gut.

Minutes later, Chicho was back and sitting by her side. She would not jump to conclusions. She'd ask Leo and let him clarify it.

Cat saw them approaching, speaking in animated tones.

"What happened?" she asked them.

"The ship was back again. I didn't see the small boat this time, but I'm nearly certain it's the same boat." He turned to Anna. "Can we find out what that boat is?"

Ann shrugged. "Not sure. I have to look into it and see if there is an equivalent to the FAA. Anything that flies is tracked on radar systems. I wonder if ships are also tracked."

Cat didn't contribute to the conversation. But she knew, without a doubt, that if a ship didn't want to be tracked, it couldn't be tracked. A captain could turn off their automatic tracking system if they wanted to.

"I wonder if that boat and whatever it's doing is related to my father's journal," Leo said.

"Interesting idea. Wonder if we can cross-reference his journal with any other data points."

Cat agreed. It was an interesting idea. But that would mean that the ships had been showing up at Fortuny Bay for decades. Doing what, she wondered?

She wanted to go to sleep, but would not, could not until all the windows and doors were locked. Even with the extra guest, she did not feel comfortable. And she wondered how she'd feel once it was just her and Chicho.

The thought gave her chills.

Chapter Thirty-Nine

Leo

Leo adjusted his tailored buttoned-down shirt. He considered the tie—with or without? He fastened the topmost button, then undid it. No tie it was. He picked up the charcoal black jacket and slid it on. Leo missed his wardrobe at home. He missed the nightlife and the ridiculous parties he'd attend. His voicemail was filled with invitations that he had ignored. But the time had come. The end was here. Soon, he'd be back to his normal life.

He stepped out of his room and descended the stairs rapidly, his leather soles tapping against the aged planks. He walked into the kitchen. Anna nursed a cup of coffee, and Chicho drank chocolate milk from a single-serving container.

"Hi," Chicho said, and raised his drink. "Momma said okay because it's ornamic."

Leo smiled. "I love ornamic," Leo said and carefully lowered himself to the chair. He didn't want to crease his clothing.

"Anna," he said.

"Leo," she said.

"I sure could use a cup of coffee."

She nodded, then sipped. "You look it."

"There was a time you made me a cup every day."

"True," she said. "That's because I was a barista, and you paid me to do it."

He shrugged. "Always arguing with facts. Maybe you should've gone to law school after all."

As he prepared his own cup of coffee, he felt her eyes on him. He turned to face her. "What?"

"How are you holding up?"

He considered her question. The truth was, he was good. He had been pissed. He had been hurt and maybe even offended, but there was no reason to believe that Cat had done anything questionable. And his investigator had discovered nothing questionable. Then again, he hadn't delivered anything whatsoever. But he presumed that no news was good news.

"Earth to Leo. Are you there?"

He snapped out of his thoughts. "Sorry. Was thinking about your question. I'm good, actually."

She grinned. "That's good to hear. So... no hard feelings?"

He studied her. "You mean with..." he shot a nod upward toward Cat's current location.

"No, with the migration patterns of swallows."

He narrowed his eyes. She'd always been a smart ass. "No, counselor. No hard feelings."

She gave him that look that said she didn't buy it. "That's good to hear. Surprising, but good."

The coffee machine chimed, telling him his cup was ready. He grabbed it and sat again. "Surprising?"

"After all these years, I have never seen you give up on something that you felt wasn't kosher. Even when the rest of us asked you to let go, even when you were in the wrong, you still went after it."

He sipped his coffee. "Point?"

"You let go of this one after, what, twenty-four hours?"

"It's a sign of maturity," he said.

"Or something else."

They stared at each other for a few long moments.

"As in...?" he asked.

She leaned in, looked toward the stairs, then lowered her voice. "As in feeling something for you know whom?"

"Feeling. Something," he said, unhappy with the insinuation.

She frowned. "Are you falling for you know who?"

"What are you guys talkin' about?" Chicho chimed in.

They both straightened. "Nothing, Chicho. We're adulting," he said.

"Adulting is confusing."

"Amen to that, Chicho," Anna said.

"Are you guys ready?" Cat said as she descended the stairs.

Leo and Anna rose. "Have been for..." he started to say, but when he saw her, the word 'ever' evaporated in his mouth.

Cat's hair was perfectly styled and combed. A touch of makeup to her eyes and cheeks, was enough to bring color back to her face. She wore a simple black one-piece dress and high-heel shoes. Cat looked—

"You look beautiful, Mama!" Chicho yelled as he ran to meet her at the base of the stairs.

The kid was spot on. But that word didn't capture it completely.

"He's right, Cat," he whispered.

Cat's cheeks immediately picked up additional tones of red. She smiled and engulfed Chicho in her embrace. "Thank you," she said.

"That's a gorgeous dress, Cat," Anna said.

She rose, straightened the dress. "Actually, and I hope you don't mind, Leo, but this was one of your mom's dresses that we were going to give away."

He shook his head. "No... this looks perfect on you."

She studied his eyes. "Thank you," she whispered.

"You should take anything of hers that you want. It's almost like they were tailored for you."

She grinned. "I may scan through the bags one more time before we give them all away. But right now, we go to the mortuary."

"To say goodbye to Mister Lionel?" Chicho asked.

She brushed his hair with her hand. "Yes. Ready?"

He nodded.

"Lola will meet us there," Cat told Leo.

She and Chicho went first. Leo and Anna were on their heels.

Again, he felt Anna's eyes on him. He faced her. Her eyebrow was arched at an impossibly high level.

He narrowed his eyes at her.

"Adulting is so much fun," Anna said, then grinned as they left the house.

The entire process was fast—transactional. The director gave them a few minutes to sit in silence with the ashes. Lola and her parents showed up. The only other person who joined them was Roberto.

Leo found this very curious. After all these years—three generations to be accurate—no one else came to pay respects? This all felt odd. Had his father's decision to take in Cat and Chicho caused rifts across all past relationships? Apparently. Either that or his angry Frenchman attitude had gotten to the rest of the community.

Still, something was wrong.

They were ushered out toward the columbaria. A term he remembered from when they took his mom's urn to the wall that housed all the others who'd been cremated. Anna was on one side and Cat on the other. Chicho stood in front of Cat, tight against her. Behind them, Lola's family. Roberto was a couple of paces away. There, but not there.

The chamber for his father was already open. Without pomp or circumstance, the usher slid his father's ashes into the chamber, then sealed it. After he did that, he lowered his head in respect.

Leo stared at the two plaques. His father's was not done yet. Soon, they told him. But his mom's plaque was there. He gazed at his mother's plaque. *Gone too soon. Devoted daughter, mother, wife.* Yes, she was.

He missed her. More than he could put into words. He remembered when she passed away. Even the Pacific Ocean mourned. The ocean sent clouds, mist, and winds, declaring a day of mourning. And that theme hung over his life until he escaped. He found relief by drowning himself in other ways.

Through his mental fog, a soft melody brought him back to the present. Cat was singing in a low voice. From the other side, Anna joined. He didn't know the lyrics, but he knew the song. It was Amazing Grace, a song he'd heard before in movies, but the words had never resonated with him.

...That saved a wretch like me...

What was this song about?

...was once blind, but now I see...

He thought of what Cat said about his father. That he had changed. Was that possible? Could a stubborn man at his age change?

Then another thought poked at him. What about him? What about Leo? Was he a wretch? Was he blind? Could there be some sort of transformation for him, too?

Suddenly, Cat clasped his hand and squeezed. He glanced at her. Tears made trails down her cheek.

He squeezed back.

Chapter Forty

Catalina

As they all walked back to the cars, Cat checked her phone. A voice mail waited for her. It was from the bank. She paused it, then put it on speaker.

"Leo, what does this mean?"

As she re-played it, Roberto and Anna also approached them.

"This is the branch manager at American Bank. Unfortunately, we've had to put a freeze or Mr. Moncrieff's account. You cannot withdraw money nor pay bills until we speak with you. Please call me back or visit us at the branch. I will be here until 6 p.m."

Cat looked at Leo. "Did we do something wrong?"

"No. We didn't do anything wrong."

"Something I can help with?" Roberto asked.

"You said you had copies of the death certificate?" Leo asked.

"Yes. They're in my car."

"Get them, please," Leo said.

Roberto opened the trunk of his Mercedes, and from his briefcase, pulled out a manilla envelope. He handed it to Leo. "Five copies."

"Thanks," Leo said, then hesitated. "Roberto, in my father's will, there's a comment about handing me his passion project."

Roberto nodded. "Yes, that's right. I remember that part."

"Do you know what this project is all about?"

Roberto shook his head. "No, not at all. I thought maybe Catalina would know."

She shook her head. "No, not me."

Leo seemed to study him. "Can you ask Maroutian? Maybe he knows?"

"Absolutely."

Leo sighed, then faced her. "Alright, let's go."

By the time they arrived back at the house to change, Chicho was out cold.

"You could leave him with me," Anna said. "I'll be working with the analysts, going through the last of the books that are still in the house."

Cat didn't like leaving Chicho behind. She didn't really know Anna. Seemed decent enough, but what choice did she have? Lola was not available.

Twenty minutes later, Cat and Leo had changed, and Chicho was taking a restful nap in Anna's RV.

They drove in silence for most of the drive. His truck's navigator showed that they were now five minutes away. She was spent and assumed he was feeling the same. These had been draining days, but it was over now. Nearly. Lionel senior was in his final resting place, and hopefully, with the paperwork that Roberto had provided, whatever was causing the issue, she hoped the bank matter would be resolved too.

She thought of what Roberto said the day before. What if this banking issue was caused by Leo? No, that didn't make sense. Why would he then jump on solving it? Then she recalled that he had someone looking into his father's death.

"Leo," she said, pulling him out of his own thoughts.

"What's up?"

She focused on his face. "Why have you hired an investigator to look into your dad's death?"

He blinked but kept his eyes on the road. "I want to know what caused his death."

She recalled the organized meds in the medicine cabinet. "Is that why you were checking out his meds?"

He glanced at her. "I'm still trying to understand what he had and how he died. I took a picture of the meds because I have someone looking into his medical history."

She hesitated. "Why keep it away from me?"

A long hesitation. "Wasn't trying to keep it from you. I figured you had plenty on your mind and—"

"Be honest with me. You know that if someone was going to collect information, I would be the right person to start with. But you didn't. Why?"

He pulled the truck into the shopping center, then eased into a spot right in front of the bank and turned off the truck's ignition.

"There are two ways to answer your question. I can spin it and it'll sound good. The other is the truth," he said.

She released the seatbelt and turned to face him. "I'd like to think that you and I can come from a place of truth."

He faced her. Took a deep breath. "I was pissed. At the will. At losing my mom's home. And at you."

"Why me? You know I didn't know... unless...." She felt her face flush.

"I was wrong. Once I calmed, I knew I'd been unfair. I know all you've ever done for him was for his best. You've been kind and generous."

"Did you think I would do something to harm him?"

"I thought a lot of things. But no, not harm him. I thought you might have manipulated him to alter the will. I had a lot of dark thoughts. I wanted to believe that this was all your doing."

"Oh, Leo..." She covered her face.

He pulled her into his chest and engulfed her in his embrace. "Forgive me. I should never have... but I was hearing things from others and then seeing odd reactions to you, and I just... I'm sorry, Cat. Sincerely."

They remained like that for a few moments. She didn't want it to end. When was the last time she felt this type of security and connectedness? Too long. But she couldn't allow this to happen. That kiss they exchanged had kept her up all night. She knew that this would end poorly. She breathed him in and was transported to another time. A time when they belonged to each other, and the world had no barriers and no obstacles. The world was wide open. The possibilities were endless. But not now.

Cat gently pushed his chest to make room. They were inches away. She stared directly into his eyes. She did not want to look at his lips. She didn't want to think about that. She didn't want him to think about that either. "You've become accustomed to the type of people that betray and double-cross. I'm not so naïve to think these things don't happen. I've seen it in my own life. I've suspected people in the past, and unfortunately, every time, they have proven—eventually—that they were not worthy of my trust. And so here we are. You and me. We don't have a good track record. I am, however, hopeful that we can get there."

"We can," he said.

"I'd like to get there. I don't have many others left in my life."

"You can trust and count on me. Plus, my dad put it in his will. So I have to be your friend."

A friend. She smiled. "Good. Now let's see what happened with the bank."

As they waited for the branch manager to arrive, Leo was furiously typing and tapping on his phone.

"What should I say?" she asked.

He tapped, typed, tapped some more. "They're the ones who have to explain. Not you. So say nothing."

"Got it," she said. "But what if they say the way I got my name on the account originally was not—"

More tapping and typing. "Don't jump to conclusions. Let them show their hand."

"Got it," she said again.

A nicely dressed middle-aged woman arrived. "Sorry to keep you waiting," she said and extended her hand to Cat. "You must be Catalina Alonzo?"

"That's right," Cat said and shook hands.

"And you are...?"

"Lionel Moncrieff," he shook her hand. He set his phone down. He was done with whatever he'd been working on.

"Oh," she said, confused.

"The son, not the elder."

"Oh, okay." She sat down, then smiled.

Silence. Cat was tempted to say something, but she saw Leo's hand gesture, indicating her to wait. She did.

"The reason for the call is that we were led to believe that there were... um... open matters with the will."

"Clarify," Leo said.

She adjusted in the seat. "Umm... As I understand it, it was not clear if Miss Alonzo did, in fact, have the authority."

"Let's make this easy," Leo said. He placed a copy of the will, the death certificate, and the notarized forms on her desk and turned them to face her. "We'd appreciate it if you release the funds ASAP and transfer them to Ms. Alonzo's account." He'd written the account number on a sticky note.

She studied the documents. "These appear to be—"

"It's not an appearance. They are certified. They are what you need."

"I will need to call our security group—"

"We're happy to wait," he said. "In the meantime, do you guys have coffee here?" He turned to Cat. "Tea or coffee?"

Her eyes widened. "Yeah, coffee would be great."

He smiled and faced the branch manager. "Two coffees while we wait would be awesome."

She straightened.

But Leo didn't let her speak. "We understand you didn't mean to disturb us during my father's funeral to give distressing news," he said. "We also know that you realized we were a good hour away, but still felt that by asking us to come here, you'd be able to resolve this. Ms. Alonzo is a widow with a five-year-old waiting for her. So let's resolve this."

She bit the inside of her cheek. "These things can't be resolved so quickly."

"Stop," he said. "You were very quick at placing a freeze on this single mother's account. It took you seconds. Earlier you said 'you were led to believe.' Your belief has been corrected. We're being reasonable. We're giving you an opportunity to release the funds."

She was turning red. "It's not that easy."

"Let me show you something." He turned on his phone and placed it in front of her. "Can you see what this is?"

She leaned in, reading whatever was on the phone. "Y... yes."

"Before I hit 'Submit,' I need this issue resolved. And as soon as that's done, we want Ms. Alonzo to get her ATM card while we're here. Also, she will need a credit card with a high credit limit. I will co-sign it."

She nodded, now with more determination. "I'm on it." She rose. "I will have someone make a run to Starbucks for you, Mr. Moncrieff."

"Perfect," he said.

She hurried away, presumably to talk to the security team privately.

"What just happened?" Cat asked.

"We're getting the money released to you, and you're getting a credit card."

"But what did you show her?"

"I showed her that I was about to open an account with her branch."

"So what? People open accounts all the time."

He leaned in. "The thing is that I don't put my money in traditional banks because all they do is take my money and loan it out and make a lot more on it. So for a small branch like this to land a client who is willing to transfer five million, well, she'll get a major bonus."

Cat's face froze. "You're going to transfer that much money? Just like that?"

"Just like that."

She shifted in her seat. "I don't like this. I'm sure I could've figured this out without having you throw your money around."

"Sure. Eventually. And how many bills would go unpaid?"

Her jaw pulsated.

"All I'm doing is speeding up the process."

"I get that. And... look, I appreciate it. But I don't want to owe anything to anyone."

"We just established that we're friends, right? Friends help each other. That's all I'm doing."

They were silent for a few moments.

"Five million..." she finally said.

"Yup."

"Must be nice," she said.

"Not gonna lie. It is."

They both broke into a belly laugh. This was something that she'd lost years ago. Laughter, security, comfort. These were all emotions that she'd forgotten and buried because she couldn't see out of the hole that she'd dug herself into. But now... maybe it was possible to believe again. And to think it was because of the one man she never thought she'd want to see again. She used to hate him. That was *not* what she felt for him anymore. No, she felt something completely different. Something potentially dangerous.

Chapter Forty-One

Leo

By the time they hit the road to return home, the sun was setting. A beautiful orange hue covered the roads as they rolled back onto the highway.

"You're not worried that I'll run up an enormous bill on the credit card?"

"No," he said without hesitation. "I know where you live."

She chuckled. "Can you call Anna? Wanna see how Chicho is doing."

He did.

"Yes, boss," Anna said. The audio came through the truck's speakers.

"Not the boss," Cat said. "How's the little guy?"

"Oh, hey. Yeah, he's great. He had some pasta an hour ago in the RV. He's getting sleepy. I'll be taking him to his room, read him a story or something."

"Thank you, thank you, thank you. We're on our way back now," Cat said.

"Did you eat?" Leo asked.

"Nope."

"Okay, we'll stop at the market and the pizzeria. Be there in under two hours," Leo said.

"Okay, no worries. I've got my laptop with me. Take your time."

They hung up and accelerated toward Fortuny Bay.

"She's amazing," Cat said.

"You ain't lyin'. She's the best. If anyone ever tries to recruit her, I will have to hire a hitman to take them out."

She didn't laugh.

"Objectively, that was funny," he said.

"Sorry, sort of sliding back into the negative headspace. Everything is so... unexpected. I'm now literally able to afford PJs for Chicho, but it's at the expense of losing your dad. And the guy that I was to hate until the second coming is picking up where his dad left off."

"I'm here. You don't have to speak about me in the third person," he said.

She chuckled, then elbowed him. "You're such a clown. How did you become so important when you're so goofy?"

"Maybe that's the difference. Maybe it's about knowing who you are, your potential, and what skills you have."

She adjusted the heater in the car. "You were always the ideas guy. A lot of bad ideas, too."

"In this game, you got to try everything, but also learn how to fail fast without holding on to dead-end ideas."

She spun to him. "Don't you mean not fail?"

"No. I mean fail fast. Most ideas will fail. If they're going to, let them fail fast. Get on the core idea quickly, develop it, test it and if the results aren't there, you kill it and move on to the next."

"Have you had a lot of failures?" she asked.

"Plenty."

A beat. "Me too. Only one success... Chicho."

He thought of their relationship all those years ago. It failed because of him. And her marriage failed because of a boating accident. External forces caused some failures. Others were your own doing. Maybe he could be the difference for her. The thought sparked a flame in his chest. He wanted to do more, be more for her.

Leo dropped Cat off at the grocery store, then drove to the pizzeria to pick up the pies he'd ordered from the road. He parked the car, hopped out, and strolled into the restaurant. The pizzas weren't quite ready.

He texted her.

Not ready. 10 more mins.

I'll come to u. Almost done.

He caught up on emails, on the status of some of the key transition activities. He also had an email from his investigator.

"Collecting medical information on hospital records," he wrote. "Following a few leads on other items."

He deleted the email. At this point, did it matter? No. Things were as they were supposed to be. No, what mattered was that Cat and Leo were in a good place. He wanted to focus on that and take it from good to great.

"Order for Leo," the guy behind the cash register called out.

He picked up the food, paid, and then returned to the truck. After he placed the boxes on the back seat, he entered the truck and noticed something on the windshield. An envelope.

He reached out and pulled it from the wiper's grip. Not addressed to anyone. He broke the seal and pulled out newspaper clippings and online articles.

He quickly flipped through them, took a deep breath, then started reading them carefully.

Fortuny Bay resident Rafael Marceli still missing at sea. It is still unclear why the twenty-six-year-old father of one took out his boat in the middle of the night when weather reports warned of rough waters for the last 48 hours. The Coast Guard said they lost track of his transponder...

He read the next one.

Foul play suspected in the boating accident that resulted in the death of Rafael Marceli, a long-time resident of Fortuny Bay. The investigators offered little information. "We are following a couple of leads," said the...

Leo's heart beat at an irregular cadence. He pulled the next one.

"Miss Catalina Alonzo Marceli is a person of interest," said the detective, investigating the death of Rafael Marceli. He stopped short of identifying the wife as the primary suspect....

This was not happening. He read the next one.

The jury could not reach a verdict. The public defense attorney called it a resounding victory for an innocent mother of a two-year-old. "We understand a grieving family. But to blame an innocent woman for a freak accident is not the answer." The family spokesperson announced that this was not the end. It was unclear if they would attempt a retrial. However...

He moved to the last one.

The battle over the custody of the four-year-old child of Catalina Alonzo continues to be a bitter issue for the family of the man who died in what some have called premeditated murder. The judge has given the mother partial custody. However, the custody will be under strict controls and measures. The mother who is accused of murdering her own husband must show the court that she is mentally and financially capable of supporting the child.

The clippings dropped on his lap.

"What the—?"

The passenger door opened. "The pizza smells so good!" Cat said as she slid into the car with two grocery bags. She placed the bags at her feet, then slammed the door. "Let's go."

He just stared at her.

"What's wrong?" she asked, then dropped her eyes to the clips. She picked one, then scanned the article. She froze. Her eyes met his. "Leo..."

"Are you about ready to come clean and tell me what the hell is going on around here?"

Chapter Forty-Two

Catalina

"What is this, Cat? What's the game?" he asked.

Her hands felt numb. Her heart thrummed in her throat. This wasn't happening.

"Well?" he asked.

"Leo, the less you know...."

"Oh no. That's not how this is going to work. I need information. Otherwise, I'm left wondering who you are. Are you the orchestrator of death? Or are you truly a victim? But when you don't give me anything, it tells me you're hiding something."

She nodded. "I am. I am absolutely hiding something. You don't know who I'm dealing with."

He leaned in. "What are you saying?"

"My life has been a constant nightmare. The nightmare started when I became a part of that family. I should've known better. But I walked into that lion's den thinking I would be a part of the family. Instead, all they've done is to do everything in their power to destroy me and take Chicho away from me."

He grabbed her shaking hand. "What happened? Just tell me."

She shook her head. "I just wish I could ask you to trust me. Believe me when I say I'm not dangerous. I'm not unstable. I'm not a risk to Chicho. Your dad knew. He took a stand against them. It became all of them against me and my small army."

He ran his hand through his hair. "Someone wants me to know that you're not who you seem to be. Someone is going to give me even more insight. You are the person who can stop this madness. Let me in."

She shook her head as tears escaped her eyes. "They'll go after you, too."

"Me?" His eyes hardened. "Are you saying they went after my dad? Is that what happened?"

She wiped at her eyes and shrugged. "I don't know."

The blaring sound of a fire truck snapped them out of their conversation. They both swiveled toward the sound in time to see a second truck speed by. Then an ambulance.

She turned to him. "Let's go home. Now!"

He threw the car in reverse and sped back, then dropped it into drive and accelerated out of the parking spot. In the distance, they could see a flickering light source. It was too dark to see smoke.

"Faster," she said.

He hammered the pedal, and they flew through the streets.

"Oh my God," she breathed.

"It may not be—" but he didn't finish the sentence. As he turned onto their street, no more maybes remained.

Casa Moncrieff was engulfed in smoke, and streaks of fire shot out of the windows. The fire trucks were rolling out their hoses. Just as Leo pulled next to the house, the water from the engines slammed against the house.

"Anna took him to his room," he said.

They jumped out of the car and raced toward the house.

"You can't go in," a firefighter yelled.

"There are two people inside," Leo yelled. "A five-year-old and an adult woman. Most likely second floor."

The firefighter ran up to another person and relayed the message. Three men who were already getting ready to run in received the message, then ran to the front door and kicked it down. Fire whooshed out of the front door.

Cat's knees gave out, and she lost her balance. Leo grabbed her and pulled her into him.

"They'll get to them," he whispered. His body tensed. "Wait. Maybe they're in the RV."

Hope filled her heart. They ran around the fire engine toward the RV. He pulled on the handle, opening the door. They both stumbled over each other into the vehicle.

"Anna! Chicho?" he yelled.

She ran toward the back, into the bedroom. Empty.

"No one's here," she said.

His shoulders slumped. "Okay, let's see if we can see anything from the back side. His bedroom window is on that side."

They ran, circumventing the firefighters. They tried to get close to the house, but the heat that it gave off was so explosive she could feel her skin chapping. Leo pulled her backward.

They froze, watching the blaze. Streams of high-powered water poured over the entire house. The constant pops and crackles became background noise.

She dropped to her knees. "Lord, please. Don't take him away. Not like this. Not now. I beg You, Father!"

He joined her on the ground, but didn't speak. He just stared at the burning structure.

"Leo!" a familiar voice yelled from behind.

They both turned toward the sound. To the backdrop of the ocean, she saw two figures illuminated by the light of the fire. Anna and Francisco.

Cat scrambled to her feet and ran faster than she'd ever run before. She stumbled over rocks and shrubs until she skidded into Chicho and lifted him off the ground, enveloping him into a tight embrace.

She spun and spun. "Thank You, Lord. Thank You, Lord." She

held Chicho like she'd never held him before. Like she would never let him go again.

Chapter Forty-Three

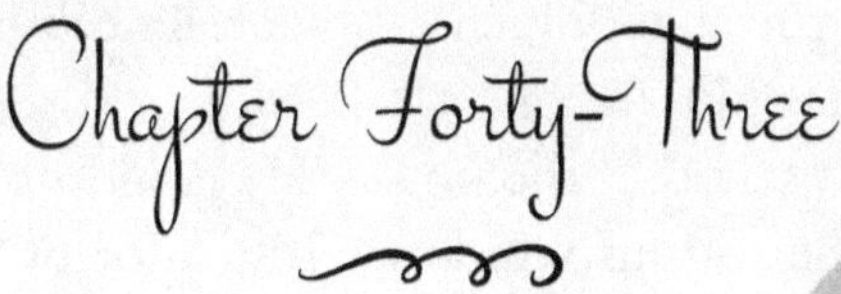

Leo

"Are you guys okay?" Leo asked as they walk toward the ambulance.

"Shaken. Some smoke inhalation. But good," Anna said. "Feeling very, very lucky."

He draped an arm around her shoulder. He'd put her in this danger. She was not the lucky one. He was.

"There's a paramedic here," he said. "Cat, take them there. They'll give them oxygen. I need to tell the firefighters to come back out. They don't need to risk their lives."

"Yeah, okay," Cat said and headed toward the van.

Leo ran toward the men on the ground while Cat ran to the paramedic's van.

"You can't be here!" a furious man yelled.

"Tell them to come back out. There is no one inside."

The man hesitated for a split second, then barked orders into his device, "I repeat. No one inside."

The first responders yelled into headsets. In less than thirty seconds, the three firefighters stumbled out of the house, all intact.

Leo left them and joined Cat, Anna, and Chicho by the paramedic. Chicho was being checked carefully. Anna wore an oxygen mask while they were monitoring her heart and blood pressure.

Cat was sitting next to Chicho, practically crushing him into her side. Anna held one of his hands.

He turned and stared at the house. He could no longer see flames shooting out of the various windows. Just a lot of white smoke. He assumed the firefighters were getting the edge over the fire. He slumped against the truck and waited.

"We're going to take you to the hospital for observation," the paramedic said.

Anna lifted her mask. "Is that necessary? I'm feeling fine."

"It's necessary," the paramedic said.

The emergency doctor allowed Leo to visit his family. Anna and Chicho were on a bed, all connected to air and probes. Cat sat in a chair next to Chicho. Her eyes bloodshot.

He knelt next to Chicho. "You alright?"

"Yeah," he said. "I wasn't scared."

"I can attest to that," Anna said. "When I was panicking, he was calm and cool."

Leo couldn't imagine Anna ever panicking.

"What happened?" he asked her.

"Shortly after I spoke with you, we went to his room. I read a really cool book. Was so into it I didn't even realize he was asleep."

Leo smiled and ruffled Chicho's hair.

"I decided to stay there on that comfy armchair. I was on my laptop and just dozed off."

Leo studied her. "You. Dozed off."

"It can happen to the best of us. It was Chicho's cough that woke me up. Smoke was already filling up the second floor."

Cat straightened. "Was an oven on? A toaster?"

"We hadn't gone into the house since we left for the funeral. We were in the RV the entire time until it was bedtime. In fact, I think the only lights that were on were the night light in Chicho's room and the front entrance light. So unless the oven took twelve hours to pop, I don't think it was anything that we'd done."

"Go on," he urged. "How'd you get out?"

"We ran," Chicho said.

"Basically, what he said. We kept low and saw that the stairs were clear."

"Through the front door?" Cat asked.

"No, kitchen. The arch toward the front was fully on fire. So we went through the back and ran into the backyard."

"Why not go to the RV?" he asked.

"We did, initially. That's how I called 9-1-1."

"You called them?" Cat asked.

"Yeah. But then, when I went outside to see the status of things, I noticed the RV's surface was very hot. So I got my hero and ran toward the ocean."

Leo leaned down and kissed the top of her head. "I am so grateful that you are you. I don't even know what to say to thank you properly."

"Fourteen days in Greece without emailing, texting, or calling me should show me how much you love me."

He laughed. "Okay, I can't promise miracles."

"I am so grateful," Cat said. "Angels ushered you two out of there. This could've been..." She didn't finish her thought.

"All the tests came back negative," the admitting doctor said. "I will discharge you soon."

They all looked at each other, relieved.

"I guess we're all sleeping in the RV now," Anna said.

"It is an enormous bed," he said.

"You get the sofa," Anna retorted.

By the time they reached Leo's car, Chicho had fallen asleep in Cat's arms. They buckled him in the booster seat. Anna and Cat sat in the back, flanking him.

They did not exchange words on the drive back. Everyone was too spent, or so Leo assumed. He certainly was.

One week ago, he had, for all intents and purposes, forgotten about this town, about this house. A few days ago, he was willing to accuse his ex of premeditated murder just to get his hands on the house. Now everything was up in the air.

What was rightfully Cat's was potentially destroyed. At a minimum, badly damaged. At least no one had been injured.

By the time they pulled up to the house, the sun was rising. Some of the firefighters were still there, putting out embers.

Leo drove the truck into the lot.

"We're here," he said, awakening the others.

"Let's put Chicho in the RV," Anna said.

Leo walked up to the fire chief while the ladies took Chicho into the RV.

"Good morning," he said.

The fire chief turned to Leo. He had deeply etched character lines. A face that said he'd given his fair share of bad news to people.

"Are you the homeowner?" he asked.

"No, she'll be right out. This was my father's until he passed away a few days ago."

He gave Leo a look that basically said, too much information, son.

Leo heard footsteps and turned to see Cat.

"Here she is."

The man nodded. "Ma'am, everyone okay? I understand your son was in the house?"

"Thank you, yes, everyone's fine. We just returned from the hospital." She hesitated, then nodded toward the house. "How bad?"

He shrugged. "Have I seen worse? Absolutely. Is it habitable? No. Not until you've had an inspector go through it all. With the right crew, it's possible. Otherwise, I would say I hope you have a good insurance provider."

Her face straightened. "I don't even know who covers this place."

"Those are just details. We'll find that information," Leo said. He knew that his father's PC was in the RV because they were going to dig through it for data. Between the history and the files that had already been saved, and Roberto, he was sure they'd find what they needed.

"How close was it?" she asked.

"Close? As in, how close of a call was it?"

She nodded.

"Hard to tell right now," he said. "But if we'd gotten the call five minutes later, then this place could've been a total loss. These old houses... on the one hand, they are sturdy, made of solid wood. On the other hand, they are made of wood that's old and dry—ideal for a fast burn. The smallest thing could set it off."

"Any idea what caused it?" Leo asked.

He shook his head. "I don't want to jump to conclusions. An investigator will look into it. But it looks like it all started from the front entrance and spread. Most of the damage is there."

Someone called the chief, who walked away.

Cat and Leo stood side by side, staring at the charred structure. The sun continued its ascent, lighting up more and more of the property. Black water ran off from the home down the dirt onto the streets. A house that had been in the family for over one hundred years now looked like a shadow of itself.

"It's all gone," Cat said. "I can't believe it."

He draped a hand over her shoulder. She leaned her head on his chest. "We just have to be grateful that no one was hurt," he said.

She breathed heavily.

"Look, I hate to be the one to say this, but the house was a bit of a mess."

She pulled away and stared at him. "Excuse me?"

"You did the best you could with what you were given. But let's be honest, the house needed a lot of work. A lot. This may be a blessing in disguise." He stopped when he saw Anna strolling toward them. "Anna, you've dealt with fire insurance, right?"

"Of course."

"They'll cover the entire house, right?"

She nodded. "Typically, yes. They'll try to give you the least amount possible, but they'll honor the terms of the policy which stipulates structure replacement, personal property, even temporary housing fees. Don't worry, we'll work them until they give you everything you need."

Leo smiled. "See? You'll be able to get the house to look amazing."

She didn't return his smile.

"Talk to me. What's on your mind?"

"I feel like I let your dad down," she said.

Leo wanted to jump in and problem solve, but knew this was not what Cat needed to hear.

She took a shaky breath in. "He entrusted me with this house. He handed me a blessing, and I allowed it to burn."

"You didn't do this," Anna said. "This is bad luck. Plain and simple. But from these ashes, you will rebuild something beautiful."

Cat turned and hugged Anna.

Chapter Forty-Four

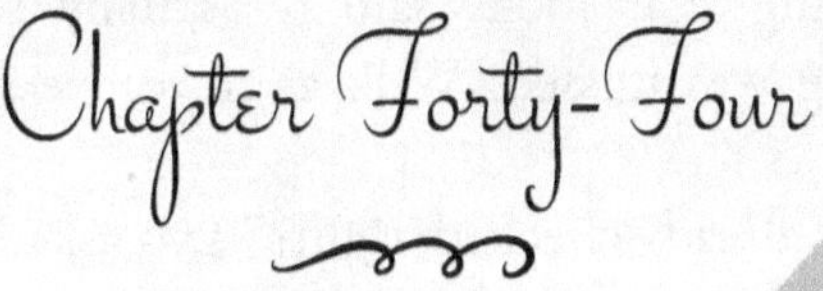

Catalina

A few hours later, the fire chief gave them the rundown.

"Cover the burnt doors and windows to protect against further weather damage and frankly unlawful entry. There are a lot of vagrants that will see this place as their new home."

"Okay," Cat said. Her head was already pounding.

"At this stage, the fire is fully extinguished. Your home is safe to enter, but as you will see, you cannot resume living in this residence. You can try to salvage items, but do not move furniture or anything heavy. Get things like glasses, medication, any clothing that's still usable. Documents like bills and bank books. Valuables like jewelry." He paused. "Questions so far?"

They all shook their heads.

"Okay, I'm gonna accompany you through the home and point out what's safe to do and what is not."

He handed each one an N95 mask. They followed him inside.

Her heart broke. Frames were destroyed. Furniture was now springs and wood. Wall paper had shriveled in some areas and was fully burnt off in other areas. Puddles of water and soot had fully ruined the floors.

She caught Leo checking out his dad's desk, which seemed to have survived most of the damage. Just mostly charred.

"The stairs have held up well," the fire chief said. "But remember, not everything that looks safe is actually safe. When inside, assume something was missed. Walk as if you're navigating a sea of eggshells."

"But you guys already checked, right?" Leo asked as he caught up to them.

"Yes, but things happen with time and weathering."

Cat took a deep breath as they reached the landing.

"The two bedrooms right above the entrance have been red taped. The floors are badly damaged, you can see right through them. Do not enter rooms with red tape."

He pointed to the master and one of the spare rooms. She was relieved that she hadn't moved a lot to the master. Just some clothes. She'd need to get toiletries. She was grateful that at least she now had money.

"Do not stay here longer than twenty to thirty minutes at a time. Go outside, get fresh air, get water, then come back again."

She made a mental note of things she'd want to get. Most were for Chicho, who was with Lola right now.

"It is important that you keep the place safe until it is fully repaired. You may even want to put temporary chain link fencing. You will want to make a comprehensive list of all things that were damaged and all things you've purchased in order to live. This will help speed up the process with the insurance."

They left the house and went back outside.

"Gas and electricity are off. Water is safe to use. I will give you a document that explains how you can get your utilities back on. Do not turn them on yourself. That could be disastrous."

"Okay..." Cat said. "Now what?"

The man shrugged. "You do your best to keep your head up and move on."

"Any idea what caused the fire?" Anna asked.

"I have an idea, but it's best that we wait for the inspector to do his full analysis and release the report."

"Was it an electrical problem?" Leo asked.

"Maybe," the fire chief said, and offered nothing more.

Cat's heat rate accelerated. She would not jump to conclusions. She couldn't afford to go down that path.

By the time Roberto pulled up, Cat and Leo had pulled out several boxes of salvaged goods and clothes. He stumbled out of the car, staring at the house, his mouth agape.

Cat approached him. "Thank you for coming here," she said. She considered shaking his hand or hugging him, but one look at her hands and clothes and she knew that was not a good idea.

"I can't believe it..." he said, his eyes fixed on the house.

"I know... each time I see the house, first I'm shocked, and then my heart breaks all over again," she said.

He shook his head, still not making eye contact with her. "For all these years, this house overlooked the rest of the town on one side and the ocean on the other side. Now..."

Leo joined them. "She'll be back," he said. "*Casa Moncrieff* will stand tall once again."

Roberto sighed. "I have been talking to the insurance company. We need to talk."

They went inside the RV. Cat, Leo, Anna and Roberto sat at the table. Lola and Chicho were at another table drawing.

"What's the matter?" Cat asked. "It was insured, right?"

"Yes," he said as he pulled a packet of papers from his briefcase. "The problem is that it wasn't sufficiently insured."

"What does that mean?" Leo asked. "Isn't there a requirement to get enough coverage?"

"Yes," Roberto said, "sort of. When you have a mortgage on the house, the bank forces proper insurance. This house hasn't had a mortgage note on it for decades. So the insurance was based on whatever the homeowner thought was sufficient."

Cat leaned back, preparing for the other shoe to drop.

"What was the coverage?"

Roberto slid on his glasses, cleared his throat, and read. "Dwelling, $137,000. Personal property, $18,000. Additional living expenses, $7,000." He slid off the lenses and looked up at her.

Cat could not produce words.

"That's impossible. My father would not have made this type of mistake. Hundred-thirty-seven grand gets you a kitchen with appliances. Not a house."

"Then again, in some parts of the country, that type of money gets you a house," Anna added.

"Okay, fine. But the insurance money is meant to repair this house. In California. Where a toilet bowl is worth five grand."

Roberto wiped his upper lip. "I... I said the same thing, so they sent me this. A fax copy of his form."

Leo grabbed the paper and analyzed the edges. He slammed it on the table. "That's cap. He has no fax machine here. Who has a fax machine these days?" He turned to Anna. "In the files we pulled, did you see anything on the fire insurance?"

She shook her head. "I don't recall. I'll search right away."

"Thanks," Leo said and handed her the sheet. "Also, look up this fax number. I want to know where this stupid machine is located."

"On it," she said as she pulled out her phone.

Cat eyed Lola, who was watching her intently. The look of pity on her face told her exactly what she needed to know. Her best friend knew Cat was screwed.

"This is unacceptable," Leo said to Roberto. "With that money, the best she can do is build a trailer. A small one. Not rebuild this home."

Roberto took out a handkerchief and wiped at his forehead. "I don't know what to tell you. This is what Lionel purchased."

"That fax number is an electronic fax," Anna said. "It's from a service where you pay for a 'scan to fax' or 'email to fax' service month by month. Does that sound like something like your dad would do?"

"Nope. He would've emailed a scanned image. That would be consistent with what we've seen from him."

"Now what?" Anna asked Roberto. "Any legal avenues?"

"The policy was renewed six months ago. Since the issue wasn't raised back then, the insurance provider will stick to its guns. What they received is binding."

"What do I do then?" Cat said. "I'm lost. I don't even know what options I have."

"If the insurance is a dead end, you can still get a loan from the bank," Anna said.

"No," Leo said. "To rebuild this place will cost at least, what, eight-hundred? Maybe a million? She can't pay that type of mortgage."

Silence.

"You could sell," Roberto offered.

Leo spun to her. All eyes were on her now. She covered her face. Was this what it all came down to? She lost the gift, and the only way to pull herself out of the mess was to sell. Was that it? Was this what it came down to?

Leo stood. "Thank you, Mr. Chaparral. We'll discuss options and then get in touch. I think we need to give Cat space to think this out."

"Can you give me the contact name at the insurance?" Anna asked. "I'd like to follow up on the details."

Roberto handed her a piece of paper with the name and number of the agent. He rose. "I am sorry that this is happening to you, Cat. If I can be of help...."

She rose and thanked him and walked him to the door.

When she closed the door, Chicho hugged her legs. "Momma, don't cry."

She hadn't realized she'd been crying. She lowered herself to his eye level. "Momma is sad, but she'll be okay. You know why?"

He shook his head.

"Because you are her sunshine."

He smiled and hugged her. She needed to get her priorities straight. Just hours ago, she thought she lost her son. And hours before that, she allowed herself to think of Leo again. No, she had to do what was right for Francisco. Everything else, including the house and Leo, were at the bottom of the list.

[illegible]

Chapter Forty-Five

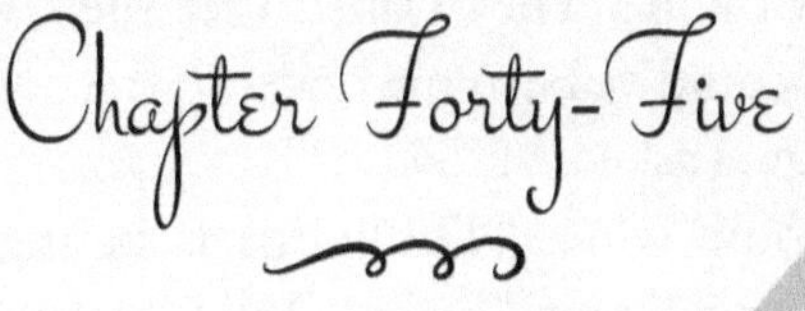

Leo

Boxes of various Italian dishes littered the table of the RV. From pasta to pizza, Cioppino to Caprese. When feeling sad, pig out. That had been Leo's motto in the early days of his start-up.

He popped the cork of the third Chianti, and more grape juice was added to their cups. Chicho had been bathed and was now fast asleep in the bedroom. Meanwhile, Anna shared funny stories, all at the expense of Leo. He didn't mind. Cat laughed until she cried and then laughed and drank some more.

He knew the art of drowning away your sorrows. He held multiple advanced degrees in that field.

They were humming to Enrique Iglesias of all things when Cat slapped the table, causing them all to jump.

"And so continues the curse on Catalina Alonzo de Marceli."

"Stop that," he said, but he knew that on some level, she was right. There had been one incident after another. This poor woman had a dark, ominous cloud hovering over her. Nothing worked for her. Not that he'd admit it to her, but even he thought it was a curse from the old country.

"It's true, Leo. I mean, look at my history. Nothing has gone right. Even my little angel is a point of contention. I'm in a never-ending battle with a family that doesn't actually want what's best for him. They want to destroy me. They want to see me... well, burnt to ashes like the house that could've been my ticket to freedom."

"Freedom?" Anna asked. "How so?"

Cat slurped some wine. "The judge is basing custody on three things." She raised one finger. "Safety. Will Chicho be safe with me? In other words, am I dangerous? Number two." A second finger popped up. "Will Chicho have a good home to live in? And three, how will I be able to provide for the boy? Do I have a job, etcetera, etcetera?"

Leo cut a slice of bread from the loaf and stuffed prosciutto inside it. "So when my father was alive, you checked off all three?"

"Yup, completely. I didn't have to have an income because your dad declared that he would cover all our expenses. And he did, to his word."

Anna added some wine to her glass. "Barring this fire business, would the judge have given you a pass?"

She shrugged. "Honestly, he was so inconsistent. I never knew what to expect from him. But logically, he should've been good with it. A safe home, free and clear of any debt. And money in the bank to cover expenses. And, of course, show that I am mentally stable." She took a sip. "I would need to land a reasonable part-time job while Chicho was in school to show that I can sustain the life."

Leo remembered something she mentioned days earlier. "But you've found it difficult to land a job here, right?"

"That's right. No one wanted to be on the wrong side of the group-think that dominates this town." Cat's phone chimed. "Who'd text me at this hour?"

"Never good news at this hour," Anna said.

She read the text, chuckled, then handed the phone to Leo.

"You read it," she said. "I've got to use the ladies room."

"Roberto," he said out loud.

"He sure has turned into the bearer of bad news," Anna said. "What's he saying?"

Leo read it again. "Dearest Catalina."

"Dearest? That's creepy."

He laughed. "Anyway. Dearest Catalina, in all this sadness, there is some good news. There is someone who wants to make an offer on your house. $750k! That would be an amazing blessing for you and Francisco. Please think about it and let me know." Leo looked up at Anna. "I'd tell Roberto to go pound sand. I love how he tries to make it sound amazing." He hesitated. "I guess depending on your perspective, it is a heck of a payday for someone who just a week ago couldn't afford to buy clothing for her kid."

Anna finished her wine. "If anyone gets this place for that price tag, they'll make a killing with the land alone and the potential. In the hands of the right person, a twenty-acre lot facing the ocean could be turned into tens of millions."

He shook his head. "You forget what you told me. In this place, the town council approves nothing. No hotels, motels, and certainly not a resort. They are stuck in their ways and in the end what this land will be is a nice single-family home."

Cat stumbled out of the bathroom. "I'm tired," she said. "No, exhausted."

Anna pulled herself up to her feet. "Come on, let's get you to bed. We all need to sleep for a few weeks."

"G'night, Leo," Cat said.

"Nighty night," he said.

She laughed and turned to Anna. "That's what he used to say to me when we were kids. And I'd say naughty night."

"Why naughty?" Anna asked.

Cat snorted. "It sounded cool. You know... Gangster!"

They both laughed, then leaned against each other as they maneuvered into the master bedroom and closed the door.

"I'll clean this up," he said. Not that anyone cared. Clearly, none of them realized how important he was.

Leo sighed, then put away the perishables and tossed the trash. He really liked this RV. He wondered how much it cost. He pushed a button, and the table moved out of the way, and the seats extended out. A nicely appointed queen bed hid under the cushion seats. He tossed those on the floor, found the storage for the pillows and blanket, and made himself comfortable.

What a day.

What a week.

He forced a smile. All was not lost. There were options, and he'd offer her a bunch of them. He frowned. Assuming she got off that pride thing of hers.

Would she consider selling? If she did, she'd walk away with serious dough. She'd be able to get a nice condo or townhouse for half of the loot and use the rest of the money to pay for life's expenses. A nice, safe middle-class life. And if she moved out of California, then she could live an upper-class life with that money. She'd never have to worry about being poor or not having enough.

He hoped that she'd weigh the options. He'd have to explain that there were real options available to her. And they started and ended with him.

He yawned. Why did all his instincts scream that something was wrong with that offer? He'd never been a God person. He was agnostic. He didn't know if there was a God, but he didn't know if there was no God, either. Maybe agnostic could also be called hedging your bets.

So was this just a series of unfortunate events or if there is a God, was he trying to teach her something? But if there was a God, could this be that other guy who introduced temptation with something as simple as an apple in the perfect paradise?

At that moment, he had a flash of the snake on the tree tempting Eve with an apple. It seemed so benign, and yet... As his mind drifted, he thought of the offer on the house. Temptation was the last thought that entered his mind before he slid into the dream world.

Chapter Forty-Six

Leo

Leo woke up early. Actually, he never really slept. So when the sun crept up, he joined the sun. He washed up, changed, then went out for a walk on the property.

He strolled through the path and reached the sand in no time. He'd forgotten how beautiful and calm this patch of beach was. The way the bay was formed, the waves that entered this area were consistent and tight—the ideal formation for surfers. He still remembered the times he spent hours here surfing. Cat would make hot dogs on his dad's grill and bring them down with bottles of Coke.

He sat on the sand. Amazed at the amount of junk he could put away in those days. His time riding the waves was where he received new ideas. Amazing ideas dropped into his head. And because of the calm that the waves delivered to his overly active brain, those ideas would flesh out. Literally, in his mind's eye, he'd see parts of the idea combine, meld, grow, and transform into something brilliant and unimaginable.

He realized now that, in some ways, he was like his mom. She would take what she saw in her mind's eye and create beautiful art. Similarly, he would take the creative ideas that he'd seen in his mind's eye and turn them into technical solutions.

Looking back, it was now clear that those were good days. He was with Cat. They were in love. Maybe all wasn't lost. Maybe.

"Hey, you," Anna called out. "Care for company?"

"Sure," he yelled back. "Who did you have in mind?"

She playfully kicked his thigh and then sat down. "Gorgeous day," she said, then took a deep breath. "This is the first time I've actually seen the rest of the property."

"Heck of a place. Wish things had been different. Wish I'd been able to have a decent relationship with my father. Wish I could've helped him renovate this place and help him find a cure to whatever it was that was slowly killing him."

Silence. "I wish I could swim like Michael Phelps."

He glanced at her. "Point?"

"Wishes are nice when you're five. At our age, we either do, or we move on and learn."

He nodded. "Anna, when you receive your award for Miss Sensitivity, I will be sure to be there... to protest."

She bumped him with her shoulder. "I reserve sensitivity for strangers. We're practically family," she said.

"You are my only family," he added.

"You need to hear things as they are sometimes. Even if it annoys you."

"And by sometimes you mean...."

"All the time."

"Clear," he said and chuckled. He took a deep breath. "I'm starting to appreciate this place."

"What do you think Cat'll do?"

He glanced at her. "She'll rebuild the house."

"Really? I'm getting the impression that she'll sell."

"No way. I won't let her do that."

She stared at him. "You won't *let* her? And what does that mean?"

"It means that selling is illogical. I'll cover her expenses that the insurance doesn't. Simple. Problem solved."

Anna adjusted herself on the sand. "What if that's not what *she* wants, Mr. Problem Solver?"

"Of course, that's what she wants. If not, I'll convince her."

She glared at him. "You need to ask her. Her! You need to listen to her. This is not one of your technical problems that you solve the way *you* want to solve it. It is not yours to solve. If—and it's a big if—she asks for options or help, then stand up and do what you've been blessed with. Otherwise, you respect her decision. And if you're itching to give her alternatives, then do so with tenderness and empathy. I barely know her, but I know this: if you try to bully her into a decision, you will lose the fight and her."

He mulled over what she said, then slowly rose. She joined him as they walked along the beach to the boulders.

"When I see the obvious, I fix it," he said.

"This one may not be yours to fix. This is her house. Her life. Her decision."

He glanced at her, unhappy with the guidance she was giving.

"Having said all that, I completely agree with you," Anna said. "She should keep the house. But I can look at a friend in a toxic relationship and say they're not right for each other. Or I can watch a friend lose himself in drinks or pretty faces and say that's destructive. But until the person in question is ready to change, nothing will make a difference."

He wasn't sure how to handle this situation. For the first time, he was like a fish out of water. They walked on, not saying much of anything. He listened to the waves, to the seagulls, and was once again surprised that there weren't more people on the beach. What was wrong with this place?

They headed back to the RV. He noticed the gate that he repaired a few days earlier was down once again. He was about to put it back up, but stopped himself.

No longer my problem, he thought. Cat would need to decide what happened with this place. Maybe Anna was right.

As they reached the RV, he kept trying to repeat what he just said. Instead, what he heard was "My problem. My problem." No, it wasn't.

But somehow, over the last few days, this house, along with Cat and Chicho, had suddenly become his problem.

They entered the RV. Cat and Chicho were also up.

"G'morning," she said. "How is it outside?"

"Pleasant," he said.

"Perfect," Anna said.

Cat sighed. "I will miss this house," she said.

Leo's heart skipped a beat. He eyed Anna. She didn't look happy but nodded in understanding.

"You're sure you want to sell?" Anna asked.

She smiled. "No," she chuckled. "Absolutely not. This place became my sanctuary for the last three years. It became the reason they couldn't steal my child right out of my hands. It became my home."

Cat sat down, and Chicho crawled into her lap.

"Just for a couple of days, I thought maybe this could be it. That it started as my safe haven, and I could realize the dream of making it a slice of heaven for people who were searching for a bed-and-breakfast."

He sat next to her.

She locked eyes with Leo. "But now... I'll never be able to complete your mom's vision for this place."

He blinked. "You mean my dad's vision."

She studied him. "No, it was your mom who wanted to do that. It had been your grandma who put the idea into your mom's head. Your dad just wanted to honor her wish. But he faced one obstacle after another with the city council. Not to mention the expense of it all."

Anna also sat next to her.

"How do you know it was my mom's idea?" Leo asked.

She glanced at him and adjusted Chicho. "Well, it was in one of the photo albums." She turned to Anna. "Do you have the one that was all lavender? It had pencil sketches on the cover of different wildflowers."

"Yeah... sounds familiar." She rose and walked over to the boxes with the photo albums in them. Leo joined her.

They went through three boxes before they found the album. He pulled it out and placed it in front of Cat on the table. She flipped a few pages, then stopped. She put her finger on a yellowed drawing that'd been placed inside the protective sheet. "There," she said.

Leo pulled the album in front of him and stared at the drawing. It was definitely his mom's drawing. He remembered this album, and he even remembered how she'd sketch with a pencil and then use pastel watercolors to give certain areas and features more depth and character.

He walked outside with the album in hand and compared the front elevation of the actual house against the drawing. The others joined him. "Looks like she wanted to add wings to the house."

"Yeah, there are some more sketches. She had ideas for how to add rooms, a sun porch. Really beautiful ideas."

He flipped through the handful of pages, digesting the work. She was amazing and creative. These few pages more than validated everything he remembered of her.

He closed the album. "Do you know where her other drawings are kept? She had oil paintings and other, larger format drawings too."

She shook her head. "No. I'm sorry. I don't recall seeing them."

A Mercedes pulled into the property. Roberto.

"Why's he here?" Leo asked.

"I asked him to come here and bring the offer letter. I figured if I'm going to make that decision, I need to be surrounded by my support team."

Roberto rushed out of his car, a piece of paper in his hand. Leo remembered the dream from the night before. A blessing? Or a temptation?

[illegible]
[illegible]
[illegible]
[illegible]
[illegible]
[illegible]

[illegible]
[illegible]

[illegible]
[illegible]

[illegible]
[illegible]
[illegible]

[illegible]
[illegible]

Chapter Forty-Seven

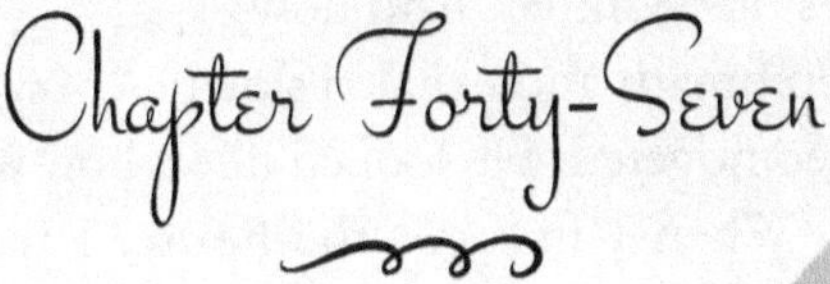

Catalina

It was an amazing offer. All-cash, ten-day close. In ten days, she'd have the money in her bank account. She'd be able to get a small place and start fresh.

"It's an amazing deal," Roberto said again.

Then why did she feel like she was about to throw up? She didn't dare look at Leo. She knew that etched on his face would be disappointment. Within a day of receiving the home—his home—it burnt down. If she'd been more responsible, then maybe today would be different. But this was her reality. She'd let Leo down.

"Who wants to buy it?" Anna asked.

Roberto looked at the name again. "Don't recognize it. Not that I'd know everyone who lives here."

"How did they hear about it so quickly?" Anna asked. "The fire just happened."

Roberto smiled. "Realtors are like vultures. When Lionel passed away, I already had been contacted."

"So, you had an offer before the fire?" Leo asked.

"Yes. But Catalina was not interested," Roberto said.

Leo turned to her, almost like he was analyzing her.

"Why would I sell?" she said. "The goal was to make *Casa Moncrieff* something extraordinary."

Leo gave her a sincere smile. "And now?"

She took a deep breath and exhaled slowly. "Maybe it wasn't meant to be," she said. Leo fidgeted. He looked like a lion wanting to pounce, but unsure how. "When I first got the house, I freaked out. I asked God, if this is from you, then align everything. Show me it's you."

"And?" Anna asked.

"It seemed like it was a blessing. All the things I was worried about got handled. You came, Leo helped, and before I knew it, things were falling into place."

"Then the fire," Leo said.

She nodded. "Then the fire. It made me wonder, maybe God was saying, hey, you misheard me. What you really need is the money and a fresh start."

Leo's shoulder's sagged.

"Like I said, maybe it wasn't meant to be," Cat said. "Maybe this is how God is communicating with me. To be honest, the whole thing, even if we had the insurance money, it's overwhelming. I wouldn't know the first thing about any of it. I have a five year old. I have a court battle. Can I really do all these things?"

Silence. Everyone's eyes were downcast. Everyone except Roberto.

"So, what do you say?" Roberto asked. "Shall I ask their realtor to draw up the official offer letter and bring it to my office?"

She took a deep breath. "Yes," she said.

"Excellent," Roberto said, more animated than she'd ever seen him. "I'll call him from the road. Let's plan to meet at say...." He glanced at his watch. "Two in the afternoon?"

Cat nodded.

He said a few more things as he left. But she heard none of it.

She breathed in, then out.

"Cat. Are you okay?" Leo asked.

She turned slightly to face him, then glanced at Anna.

She controlled her emotions. She willed her tears to stay where they belonged—inside. All on the inside.

She had no choice.

She had to live to fight another day.

Cat took Chicho's hand and joined the others, who were already outside in front of the house. Anna had prepared sangria for the adults and lemonade for Chicho. Five lawn chairs had been placed in what would've been the backyard, facing the house.

They each took a drink and sat down. The pungent smell of burnt wood and damp soil had not left the grounds.

"This feels surreal," Cat said. "Like I'm watching a movie. Because it can't be real that this house that in some ways symbolized this town is now destroyed."

A breeze came through and the smell of the charred wood momentarily disappeared.

"I can't believe I allowed this to happen," Cat said.

"Don't be so hard on yourself," Lola said. "It's a freak accident."

Cat eyed her. Was she right? Maybe. "We can all say what we know is true. We are all disappointed. I failed. I should've protected this house. But I failed the house. I failed the family."

"You really need to stop that," Leo said.

"Seriously," Lola added.

"When can I go back to my room, Mama?" Chicho asked.

"We won't be living here anymore," she said. "We'll get a new place."

Chicho's brows furled. "But I like mister Lionel's house."

"I do too. But because of the fire, we can't live here anymore."

"Ohh..." Chicho said, then looked at the house. "Are we going to live on the bus?"

Anna chuckled.

"No, we'll get our own place."

"Ohh..." Chicho repeated. "Who is going to live with us?"

"Just us."

Chicho turned to Lola. "Do you want to live with us?"

She grinned. "I'll be going back to my house soon."

Chicho turned to Anna. "How about you?"

Anna smiled.

"Sweetie," Cat said. "Just me and you."

Chicho took a sip of his lemonade and seemed to consider the situation.

"Where will you move to?" Anna asked. "Ten-day close doesn't give you a lot of time. Have you looked?"

Something occurred to Cat. "No, I haven't looked, but... what if I can't find a landlord who'll rent to me?"

"What about a townhouse?" Leo asked.

Lola laughed. "Townhouse? Here? They haven't approved new development in years. It's either an apartment in one of the few complexes here, or a lower-priced house."

"How about outside of town?" Anna asked. "More options, even 30 minutes out."

"I can't have Chicho outside of Fortuny Bay. Court order."

"So... if you got a place outside, he can't stay with you?" Anna asked.

"Not until the court ends this craziness."

Silence. She drank the last of the sangria and rose. "I say we go and eat at the diner—the only place that will serve me. And then finish the deal with Roberto and the buyer."

They all rose.

A thought dawned on her. "It wouldn't surprise me if the buyers were really from Raf's family," she said to no one in particular. "With that family, anything is possible."

Chapter Forty-Eight

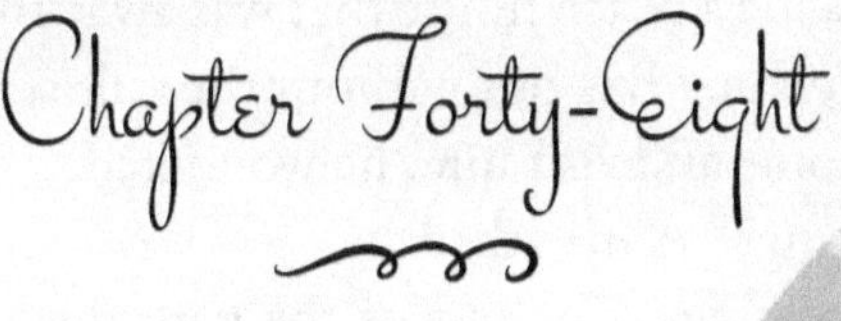

Leo

Leo ate a French fry here and there. Chewed some salad and drank the Arnold Palmer. But he had no appetite. He really and desperately wanted the day to be over. He wanted to head back home. He wanted to get himself lost in something else and not think about this town, the house, and Cat. But he didn't want to leave. He didn't want to be away from her.

He pushed those thoughts away and reminded himself that she still needed help. When he was about to announce that he'd be heading back home, Anna had said that she'd stay a bit longer to help Cat find a place.

If she found a place, he thought.

Not my problem, he thought. And it wasn't. He'd done a lot to help her and Chicho. No objective person would argue that point. And given her explanation, how could he try to tell her that what she felt was wrong?

Adulting really did suck. He preferred creating new things.

Launching impossible ideas. He even missed the parties, the drinks, the women, the music.

Did he? Maybe a little. He knew now that he had to find a balance. This life—the beach life was something that had always been important to him. Instead of buying a place in Chicago or Paris, maybe he'd find a lake house. Or maybe a beach house that was away from the city.

A place like Fortuny Bay but without the cultist weirdos of Fortuny Bay. Would Cat come and visit him, he wondered.

"Are you coming?" Anna asked.

He looked up at her. The rest of the party had already slid out of the booth. He'd been completely lost in his own world.

"Yeah, yeah," he said and followed them out of the diner.

In five minutes, they were back in Roberto's office. Lola stayed in the reception area with Chicho. Anna, Leo, and Cat entered the office.

"Come in, come in," Roberto said. He was as happy as Leo had seen this man.

What's his cut? Leo wondered.

"Here's the offer letter. Please check it for accuracy. I already did, but make sure it all looks good."

Cat started reading it, and Anna joined her. They asked clarifying questions while Leo sat in the corner sulking.

Blessing or temptation?

What in the world was he thinking about? What did that even mean? Cat was about to get three-quarters of a million dollars. It was a stinking blessing.

He remembered the letter his father left him for the will reading. What was it he wrote? 'You don't need more things. You need a home.'

You need a home.

Leo didn't want someone whose surname was not Moncrieff to live in that house. A Moncrieff had gifted it to Cat. That's what was supposed to happen.

He dropped his hand on the document. "No," he said.

They all looked at him. Roberto's eyes went wide. Cat spun to him, confused. Anna watched him intently.

"We're not signing this," he said.

"We're not?" Cat asked.

"No, we're not."

"Leo, please, it's hard enough. I will not negotiate and get into an endless back and forth. It's time to move on. It just wasn't meant to be."

He grabbed her arm and lifted her to her feet. "First, stop saying that. Second, come with me," he said. "Anna, that document goes nowhere until we're back."

"Done," she said and crossed her arms.

"Leo, Cat, please. This is highly unorthodox," Roberto said.

"Completely agree with you," Leo said. He pulled her out of the office, out of the reception area—Lola, the receptionist, and Chicho watched them go by—and down the stairs to the outdoors.

"Leo, what are you doing?"

"Hold on. Just bear with me. Don't go upstairs and don't sign anything. Just wait here. Three minutes."

"Three."

"Maybe five."

She sighed. He didn't care. He had to make a call.

"Perfect," he said into his receiver. "Thank you. You totally came through."

He hung up, grabbed her arm again, and pulled her upstairs. They strode into the reception area—Lola, the receptionist, and Chicho watched them in confusion—and went back into Roberto's office.

"Good, you're back," Roberto said. "Can we finish this? Cat?"

"Here's my offer," Leo said.

"Your offer?" Roberto and Cat asked at the same time.

"Cat, tear up that contract," Leo said.

"What?" Cat asked. "What are you talking about?"

"You're not selling to these yahoos. If you were to sell it to anyone, the only person you should consider is me."

She flinched. "Oh. I never even thought..."

"Because you shouldn't have to think about that. This is your home. You have a bed-and-breakfast to build. And I know, without a doubt, that if my mom or dad were alive, they would not sit here idle as you gave away their dream."

Tears welled her eyes. "What are you saying?"

"Let's go!" Anna yelled, scaring Roberto.

"They gave you their dream. They didn't give it to me. He knew I had the money to just throw at it, walk away for a year, and come back to a perfect place. My heart would not be in it. My dad recognized your heart when we were fifteen. He saw in you what this house needed."

She wiped at her eyes.

"I just spoke to the bank. The money I deposited in their branch a couple of days ago is now a linked account to yours. That money is yours to use however you see fit. Build the bed-and-breakfast. This is not a loan. It's a gift."

She remained frozen, staring at him.

"Okay," he said. "Let me try it this way. As Anna can attest, I don't know much about God. But my instinct is that God does not destroy things. Particularly dreams. He creates. He wants you to create. And maybe I'm being used to help you make it happen. I believe that you'll find it inside you to create my mom's vision."

Her cheeks were red. Her eyes, red-rimmed.

"You're killing me, Cat. What do you say?" he asked.

"I... I can't."

Anna slammed the table. "Oh yes, you can! Say yes," Anna yelled.

Leo trained his eyes on Cat's and then held her by her shoulders. "It's what you want. It's what you were willing to do, even when you had no financial means. Now you do."

Her mouth opened to speak, hesitated, then tried again. "How can I ever repay this—?"

"You don't repay gifts. You receive them. A gift has no expectations attached to it. Otherwise, it's not a gift."

"Catalina," Roberto interjected. "Do you even know where to start with rebuilding a house? Clearly, this is a very generous offer, but if it chains you down, it may feel like a... like a...."

"A curse?" she asked, never moving her eyes off of Leo's.

"Maybe, yes," Roberto said.

"No. Now I'm sure. This one is a blessing. Thank you, Leo," she said and hugged him. He returned the hug. This was how it was supposed to be. Her in his arms. To him, this was perfect. Did she feel the same? Did she want this, too? Or was he alone in this one?

Maybe this way, by rebuilding the house, they could trust each other again, like each other again, fall in love all over again. Why not?

A tearing sound caused them to pull away from each other.

It was Anna. Tearing up the agreement. "Let's celebrate," she said.

Leo turned to Roberto. "I'm sorry about this."

Roberto shrugged, then smiled. "I am certain the place will be beautiful."

Chapter Forty-Nine

Leo

The entire team hovered behind Leo's tailgate. On it, they had laid out his mom's drawings.

"It will be absolutely beautiful," Lola said. "I can't believe you're really going to do this."

"We are," Cat said.

"No, Cat," Leo said. "This is your house. Your project. I will not get in the way. If you want my opinion about this or that, cool. But I meant it when I said you can do whatever you want."

She shook her head. "Is this real? Is this my life or just an amazing dream?"

"No dream," Anna said. "It's all real. Now, not to be the party pooper, but—"

Chicho started laughing uncontrollably.

"What's up with you?" Leo asked.

He laughed as he pointed to Anna.

"Deep breath, now talk."

"She said poop!"

"Dear Lord," Lola said. "A poop joke."

"What were you going to say?" Cat asked.

"You will need to get an architect and a builder. You still need to coordinate with the insurance. And you will need to live somewhere while this place is being built."

"Right," Cat said. "Maybe the insurance can help with some of that. I don't know."

"Just like we did before, you're going to create a list of things that you need to do. Prioritize them and go after them. Don't let the details drive you. You drive the details."

"We need to create motivational posters—thoughts by Leo," Lola said.

"Anna, maybe the place where you rented this beast has similar things that are more long-term," Leo said.

"Sure, I'll..." she stopped talking as her attention drifted to behind Leo.

They all turned. A squad car and another car pulled up.

Cat walked toward the cars, and Leo followed her. Billy slid out of his car, so did his partner. From the second car, two women came out.

"What's going on, Billy?" Leo asked.

"Catalina, here is a summons by the honorable Judge McAuliffe. We are here to take Francisco Marceli into protective custody."

"What? No!" Cat yelled. "Ms. Davenport, why? What happened?"

The lady in gray pants approached Cat, but more to stop her from getting in the way. "Catalina, this will all be sorted out. But right now, we have to do the right thing for Francisco."

Was she a social worker, Leo wondered.

"Billy, what are you talking about? Why?" Leo asked.

"Leo, please step back," the deputy said.

"Mama, what are they doing?" Chicho cried as the other woman hovered around him, trying to coax him into going with them.

"She has a right to know why," Anna demanded. "Explain why?"

"For child neglect and endangerment," Davenport said.

"That's a bunch of crap," Lola said. "Francisco gets exactly what a child needs from his mom. He's not in danger."

"Lola, mind your own business. Cat will receive the results of the fire inspector's analysis," Billy said. "Plenty of concerning findings."

Chicho escaped their grasp and ran into his mother's arms. "Don't let them, Mama!"

"Hand him over, Cat," Billy said. His hand rested on his handgun.

"Billy," Leo said. "Are you serious right now? You are putting your hand on your sidearm? What the hell—?"

"Unless you want me to haul your ass in also, I'd keep my mouth shut."

Leo's eyes bore in on him. A thousand decisions were made at that moment.

The tears, the cries, the supplications, and the demands all got mixed in. All Leo saw was red. This was not right. This was dirty business.

Cat fell to her knees as the cars drove off, leaving behind a cloud of dust, rubble, and tears.

Leo gently pulled her up and into his arms. "I will not let them do this. This is not over."

She shook her head. "You still don't understand," she said through tears. He helped her up to her feet. Anna and Lola helped walk her to the truck.

"What's going on?" Anna asked. "Why is all this happening?"

"Because," Lola started, "that family has influence, and they use it."

"Then we fight back," Leo said.

"Don't you see?" Cat asked, as she wiped her face. "The more I fight, the worse things get."

"But if the facts and the truth are on our side—" Leo started to say.

"Truth? Since when has that mattered? You don't understand who we're dealing with. You have no idea what they're capable of. My only hope is for the judge to hear my side. So far, they've convinced him to grant everything they want."

Silence. Anna dropped on the tailgate next to Cat.

"What now?" Anna asked.

"A court hearing which will be granted immediately. The social worker will probably make the case that my sweet Chicho will be better served if he's with his grandparents because of the fire. And the judge will most likely agree."

More silence.

"Then what?"

Cat looked up at the sky. Fresh tears streaked down her cheek. "Check mate. They have always wanted sole custody. Best I can pray for is visitation."

"No," Leo said. "That's bull—"

"Yes, Leo," she said as she bore into his eyes. "This is *my* reality." She covered her face. "I wish I had known they'd take him today. I would've held him longer. Kissed him more. Spoken to his heart to make sure he never forgets me."

"This isn't over, Cat. We'll fight," Lola said.

"What if I brought in some influence of our own? What if I asked Adela Roca to help?"

"Adela?" Lola said, the indignation in her voice unmistakable.

"What are you talking about? Don't you know?" Cat asked. "Raf's mom is Elizabeta Roca. Raf was Adela's grandson."

Suddenly, everything made sense. She'd been moving the chess pieces all along. What had she told her at the bar?

When it comes to my children and grandchildren, I have a blind spot. I accept that and gladly accept all that comes with that.

Cat swiped at her cheeks, wiping the tears. "I should've realized that this battle was over three years ago. But I kept believing and hoping. And now... I don't know if I can win this fight."

Leo took her hand in his. She glanced at their intertwined hands, then looked up into his eyes.

"I don't believe in no-win scenarios," Leo said as he stared at the tire tracks left by Billy and the social workers. "It's just a matter of deciding what we're willing to do to get the victory."

He turned to face her and squeezed her hand. Cat blinked. "What are you saying?"

"I am here with you. You are not alone. You are not outnumbered.

They were the ones who decided to play dirty. They established the rules. We'll play by their rules."

—The End... For Now—

*Continue the series with **Secrets of Fortuny Bay**, Book 2 in the Fortuny Bay series. Secrets concludes this duet series.*

Please Leave a Review!

If you enjoyed this book, you can make a big difference by leaving a review.

Honest reviews of my books help in getting the attention of new readers.

To leave a review, return to the retailer's website, search for REUNION AT FORTUNY BAY, and leave an honest review.

Thank you!

Join Ara's V.I.P. Club

Ara Grigorian's VIP Club members receive free behind the scenes content to accompany the book.

Members are always the first to hear about Ara's new books and publications.

Click to Join my VIP Club:
www.AraGrigorian.com

Books by Ara Grigorian

Second Chance Coast Series

Game of Love

Ten Year Dance

15 Days With You

***

Fortuny Bay Series

Reunion at Fortuny Bay

Secrets of Fortuny Bay

Author's Notes

For those who've read my previous novels, the name "Fortuny" may spark a memory. Okay, I'll help. In *Game of Love*, near the very end, Gemma goes on the hunt to find Andre. She goes to Barcelona to a little beach town named Vilafortuny.

Vilafortuny is real. That was where we had our summer home when I was younger. We had this cool little beach house where we spent all our summers.

Fortuny Bay is not real. But it could be.

When I travel—small road trips or across the Atlantic—I study those off the map small towns. Those places that are there, but almost in the shadows. People live there. They make a life there. Somehow... and that's when my imagination takes over. What happens there? What stories can be unearthed? What secrets have been buried there for generations?

Fortuny Bay is one of those places.

This is the first book in the Fortuny Bay series. I hope Cat and Leo have grown on you. I also hope you're rooting for Chicho, because I know I am! I also hope that you see, there's more to this town—to these people—than meets the eye.

One secret between us — I don't know everything they're up to either. I'm allowing the characters reveal the story. I look forward to seeing what they're all up to.

The next novel will be released later in 2022. Thank you for joining me on this ride.

Acknowledgments

It doesn't get easier. I'd argue that it gets harder. And to make it in this jungle that is part creative, part technical, part entrepreneurial, what all authors need is a team.

Stacey Donaghy is more than just an agent. She is a source of encouragement and guidance. Above all, she is a friend.

My wife, Delia, understands her role as my first reader: tell me truth, encourage me, keep me humble. She is VERY successful in all areas.

My beta readers who take on my raw manuscripts and help me make them better: Andreh Anderson and Janis Thomas. I can't thank you enough.

Janis Thomas — not sure what I did to deserve your friendship. But I'm sure glad I did it. Thank you for all that you do for me.

Jean Jenkins... I miss you. I know you're in heaven. And I know you're using your gifts in heaven — writing, reading, and helping.

My cover designer, Tracy Van Dolder of Virtually Possible Designs. You have become more than a cover designer. You are a trusted friend and my sister in Christ. I know has my back. What I don't know is what other surprises you have up your sleeve. God has blessed you mightily. Thank you for who you are!

My childhood friend, Armen Melik-Abramians of FlashCube Photography — thank you! I do wish you would use a bit more photoshop and change my face into someone else's. Until then, I am grateful for the photos.

The wolfpack: Norm Thoeming, Trey Dowell, and Chase Moore. Neither time, nor distance can weaken the bond we have.

Michael Steven Gregory of the Southern California Writers'

Conference (Irvine and San Diego): Thank you for always having the door open for me to teach. Thank you for trusting me with your conferees. Thank you for being who you are. A special thank you to the staff, to the volunteers, and the workshop leaders — you make us all better.

My friends and family: I love you.

To my fans: I love you, too!

Fight the good fight!

Author's photo courtesy of FlashCube Photography © 2021

Ara Grigorian is a USA Today Bestselling author whose novels include the international award-winning Game of Love, Ten Year Dance, 15 Days With You, Desire After Dark (anthology), and Reunion at Fortuny Bay, his latest series. Fascinated by the human species, Ara writes about choices, relationships, and second chances. Always a sucker for a hopeful ending, he writes contemporary stories targeted to adult and new adult readers.

Ara is also a technology executive in the entertainment industry. He earned his Master's in Business Administration from University of Southern California. True to the Hollywood life, Ara wrote for a children's television pilot that could have made him rich (but didn't) and nearly sold a video game to a major publisher (who closed shop days later). Ara and his wife are the proud parents of two teenage boys and two senior cats. They have laid roots in both Los Angeles and North Dallas.

Ara is a story coach and a workshop leader. He has taught at the Southern California Writers' Conference, Santa Barbara Writers Conference, and the Writer's Digest Novel Writing Conference.

Ara is represented by Stacey Donaghy of Donaghy Literary Agency.

www.AraGrigorian.com